# Fighting Blind

Reeves raised the knife and charged.

Fargo jumped aside at the last moment, grabbing the man as the last of the firelight snuffed out. Now they were in the dark, struggling on the cold stone floor of the cavern, their hands locked on the knife, rolling hard against the rocky ground. Wincing with pain, Fargo threw his injured leg over Reeves's hip, locked it, and twisted with all his might. And then suddenly Reeves was gone. Vanished into the black of the underground night.

Fargo held his breath, listening.

And then he heard a dry rasp of air, an insane cry of rage, and the thud of bootsteps. He spun around just as Reeves bulled into him, slamming him into the wall, and bringing the knife down in a brutal arc toward Fargo's heart. . . .

# THE
# TRAILSMAN
#219

# ARIZONA
# SILVER
# STRIKE

by

## Jon Sharpe

A SIGNET BOOK

SIGNET
Published by New American Library, a division of
Penguin Putnam Inc., 375 Hudson Street,
New York, New York 10014, U.S.A.
Penguin Books Ltd, 27 Wrights Lane,
London W8 5TZ, England
Penguin Books Australia Ltd, Ringwood,
Victoria, Australia
Penguin Books Canada Ltd, 10 Alcorn Avenue,
Toronto, Ontario, Canada M4V 3B2
Penguin Books (N.Z.) Ltd, 182–190 Wairau Road,
Auckland 10, New Zealand

Penguin Books Ltd, Registered Offices:
Harmondsworth, Middlesex, England

First published by Signet, an imprint of New American Library,
a division of Penguin Putnam Inc.

First Printing, January 2000
10  9  8  7  6  5  4  3  2  1

The first chapter of this book originally appeared in *Pecos Belle Brigade*,
the two hundred eighteenth volume of this series.

Printed in the United States of America

PUBLISHER'S NOTE
This is a work of fiction. Names, characters, places, and incidents either
are the product of the author's imagination or are used fictitiously,
and any resemblance to actual persons, living or dead, events, business
establishments, or locales is entirely coincidental.

# The Trailsman

Beginnings . . . they bend the tree and they mark the man. Skye Fargo was born when he was eighteen. Terror was his midwife, vengeance his first cry. Killing spawned Skye Fargo, ruthless, cold-blooded murder. Out of the acrid smoke of gunpowder still hanging in the air, he rose, cried out a promise never forgotten.

The Trailsman they began to call him all across the West: searcher, scout, hunter, the man who could see where others only looked, his skills for hire but not his soul, the man who lived each day to the fullest, yet trailed each tomorrow. Skye Fargo, the Trailsman, the seeker who could take the wildness of a land and the wanting of a woman and make them his own.

*Arizona, 1860, where the promise of the mother lode wafts sweet in the desert air, mingling with the scents of spilled blood and burnt powder. . . .*

# 1

"I said, get down the shaft!"

The girl put her two fisted hands on her hips. "Daddy, you're going to have to stop acting like I'm seven! I can shoot, you know! Whoever's out there, I can sink a lead ball between his—"

"*Now,* Clementine!" he roared, and the girl, twenty-two years old and just as stubborn and strong-willed as her mother had been, rolled her eyes a last time.

She retreated into the mine's mouth with a "Hmph!" just as a slug sang off the rock face beside him. Tell McBride ducked, but as he did, he noticed that his daughter picked up a little speed.

*Good,* he thought with a smile, then turned to business. Tell called out to his brother, Tyrone, who was hunkered down behind a careless pile of boulders, his eye fairly glued to the sites of his long gun. "You see him?"

"No, dammit!" Tyrone replied, lifting his gaze from the sites only long enough to spit out a brown stream of tobacco juice. "He were just down there, by the waterhole, in that clump of paloverde. Got half a mind to just start pepperin' it again."

"Not unless you got as good a nose for lead as you do for silver," Tell warned. "We ain't got but six slugs left between us, and no more to melt and mold till we go to town again."

Tell knelt beside his brother, and they both

searched the brush, looking for the smallest signs of motion. "Don't know why you had to take a potshot at that feller, anyhow, Tyrone," he said, disgusted. "Probably would'a just watered that fancy horse a'his and moved on, and never would'a knowed we was here! Six slugs ain't gonna do us no good if we're beset by Apaches."

Tyrone growled something under his breath that Tell didn't quite catch, although it was likely something about younger brothers being seen and not heard—even if that brother was only two summers younger and fifty-three years old. Between an uppity daughter and a bossy older brother turning him this way and that, fairly banging him over the head with words, Tell figured it was a pure miracle they hadn't driven him into the ground like a corkscrew.

"There!" hissed Tyrone, shifting the barrel of his long gun slightly and pointing. "Reckon I should chance a shot?"

"All of a sudden you're askin' me?" By this time, Tell had taken up his old flintlock. Tyrone always sneered at it, called it fit for nothing but the trash heap, but it had been their daddy's. It had served him well enough during the War of 1812, and Tell didn't have any reason to believe it wouldn't continue to take care of him and his own.

Tyrone scowled. "Well, you're the one complainin' about the lead shortage. Ain't seen a single Apache the whole dang time we been working this diggin', anyhow." He paused, squinting along the barrel. "Crikey! He ain't fired but that one time, and I can't even see his horse no more! Now, how can a whole, big, loud-colored horse just disappear? What'd he do? Put it down a gopher hole?"

"Close, but no cigar."

Both men wheeled at the new voice, which came from the rise at their backs. Someone stood on the slope above the mine shaft: a tall man, lank, and with a close-cropped beard. A Henry rifle glinted dully in his hands, and by the look of him, he could probably do quite a bit of damage with or without it. He looked more annoyed than mad, which promised to be, so far as Tell was concerned, a blessing.

The man shook his head, and said, "You boys want to lay down those arms and tell me just why the hell you were shooting at me?"

Once he'd collected the men's firearms and ascertained they were the only souls in camp, Skye Fargo whistled for the Ovaro. The horse, a tall and well-made black-and-white paint, rose from behind a clump of mesquite, shook the dust from his gleaming hide, and moseyed toward them.

"Crikey," breathed one of the old codgers. "Dang horse does tricks."

They were a couple of rock-breakers, by the look of them. Dust lay thick on their trousers, shirts, and boots and had worked into their creased faces, as if they spent their days and nights burrowing underground. Their picks and shovels and other equipment—if such existed—were hidden away, but Fargo didn't care to snoop for them. If, indeed, there was a mine, it was their business. He just didn't like people taking potshots at him.

He leaned his Henry against a rock and crossed his arms. "You boys got names?" he asked.

"Puddin' Tame," said the taller of the two. "Ask me again and I'll tell you the same."

The other one rolled his eyes. "I'm Tell McBride, and this here smart apple would be my brother, Tyrone. And who might you be?"

"Name's Fargo," he said, extending his hand. "Skye Fargo."

He'd already decided these boys weren't the type to kill. They'd just got a little nervous, that was all. Living alone in the desert could do that to a fellow.

Tell took his outstretched hand and gave it a firm shake. "Say, I believe I've heard'a you! You the one they call the Trailsman?"

Fargo nodded. "Guilty. I'm on my way to Jupiter. September Downy asked me to mail a letter for him."

Tyrone, who still hadn't shaken his hand, arched a brow. "You say you're a friend of Sept's?"

Fargo nodded. "His p.ace is a far piece from no-where and anywhere. Been riding three days and haven't seen fresh water since the Flatheads. Sorry if that spring down there is private property. I had no intention to trespass."

Tyrone, his face still wadded into a scowl, said, "Well, Jupiter's just a hop, skip, and a jump down the road. You can make 'er in three hours if you leave now."

"Uncle Tyrone!" said a new—and distinctly fe-male—voice. "Where are your manners?"

All three men turned toward the far edge of the boulders, and there stood the prettiest girl Skye Fargo had seen in a month of Sundays.

Glossy hair so dark brown it was nearly black was pulled back at the nape of her neck, and shorter strands waved around her face like fairy curls. Her face, even-featured with long-lashed, pale blue eyes, was tanned to gold by the sun.

She was lush of breast and hip, and slim of waist, and her long legs were clad in trousers which were considerably cleaner—and considerably better filled out—than those of her uncle Tyrone. Her full bosom strained against the bone buttons of the man's shirt she wore.

"Gol-dang it, Clementine!" Tell said, and slapped his leg with his floppy hat, exposing a bald head fringed with curly salt-and-pepper hair. "I thought I told you to stay hid until we saw what was what!"

She cocked her head. "I thought you already knew

4

that, Daddy," she said with a smile aimed at nobody but Fargo.

He smiled back. She was like a rose grown up in a briar patch.

"We have a guest," she continued, "and a famous one, too, if I'm to listen to you. Mr. Fargo, I should like to apologize for my father and my uncle. Not only was it rude to shoot at you, but we can scarcely afford the expenditure of ammunition. Would you care to join us for a cup of coffee?"

"Crikey!" exclaimed Tyrone in obvious exasperation. "Why did you ever send her to Boston-town for anyhow, Tell?"

"Beats the holy pee-waddin' out of me," Tell muttered as they all obediently trooped along behind Clementine, down into a hollow hidden from view of the rocks and the spring, where the brothers had made their campsite.

All the way down, Fargo was watching Clementine's little backside swish back and forth in those pants.

Tempting. Very tempting.

# 2

"Skye? Skye, honey? You sleepin'?"

It was dark. The only light in the room came from a lamp turned down nearly to gutter, and it took him a second to realize that he was in a feather bed instead of a blanket over the cold ground, that there was a roof between him and the stars, and that it was Blond Alice who was talking.

At least, he thought he remembered that was her name.

He tried to ask what she wanted, but it came out, "Umph?"

"Oh, goodie!" she breathed against his ear. "You're awake. What'ya say we go round again, baby? No charge this time, okay?"

Since her hand had curled over his hip and was grasping his stiffening member by the time she said "No charge," and since, by that time, he'd managed to remember that he was in the town of Jupiter, at the Palace Hotel, and that Blond Alice was an overage but eager, dimpled blonde with an impressive chest and even more impressive lovemaking skills, he rolled toward her.

"Anything you say, darlin'."

Giggling, she swept back the bedclothes. He was already fully erect and she straddled him, slowly easing herself down upon him inch by inch. It was too slow for his taste—after all, when you woke a man up out of a sound sleep, the least you could do was get to business.

So he put his hands on her hips and pushed her down all the way, burying himself in her warmth.

She got the message. She let out a pleased sigh and swirled her hips, then began to pump up and down in earnest, her eyes closed and her mouth open.

He took her breasts—golden orbs in the dim lamplight—into his hands and teased at the nipples, rolling them, pinching them gently until they were hard, then palming them, letting his fingers splay back to her sides.

Eyes still closed, her hips still pumping rhythmically, she lowered her torso to his and whispered, "Do me, Skye, do me now, okay? The way you did last night."

He took his cue, rolling her onto her back without losing contact.

He was fully awake by this time. Deftly, he pulled up one of her legs, then the other, so that her knees were over his shoulders and she was completely open to him. He pushed himself into her more deeply. Her reaction was a high-pitched whimper of delight.

Now he began to stroke deeply in and out of her, slow and strong, then faster, with almost punishing depth. She was slick and tight around him, and he saw the shadows of her hands start to twist the bedclothes.

He felt her back arching at the same moment that he felt the heat in his loins pulsing to the pitch he knew would bring imminent release.

He gritted his teeth and tried to think about something, anything other than what he was doing, but then she cried out his name, and he let himself go over the edge, too, pumping deep inside her with three final erupting thrusts.

He fell back upon his pillow, spent, and they lay there for a moment, not moving. What time was it anyway? he wondered drowsily—and somewhat belatedly. The window showed a sky as dark as the inside of a black sow.

He was just groping along the nightstand for his pocket watch when Alice cuddled up against him and said in her husky little voice, "Skye? Nobody's ever done me like you do. That's the truth, baby. Nobody. Most'a these cowpokes just wanna stick it in me every which-way, and they don't give a rat's behind how I feel about it. You're a true gentleman."

"And you, Alice," he replied, "are an oasis in the Sahara."

It was true. He'd come a far piece with not a skirt in sight until he'd come across Clementine McBride. Unfortunately, he'd come across her father and uncle, too, and by the time he'd downed half a pot of coffee and had ridden to town, just the thought of Clementine—and the way her backside moved in those tight, tan britches and the way those light blue eyes burned cool out of her face—had made him peach orchard crazy.

Alice wasn't Clementine, not by a long shot, but she'd surely do.

"I'm a what?" Alice asked, unsure as to whether she'd been insulted.

Fargo's arm went round her shoulders and he gave her a hug. "It means that you're water to a thirsty man, darlin'."

"Oh," she said, and sighing happily, snuggled closer.

Fargo reached for his watch and held it in front of his face, squinting. "Two o'clock?" He turned it, trying to catch what little lamplight there was. Yes, he'd read it right. "Alice, do you have any idea what time it is?"

"Um," she breathed.

"Oh, well." He sighed, and closed his eyes. Alice was happy, he was sated, and he could always catch up on his sleep.

Of course, he didn't count on Alice waking him again at four. And at six.

At eight o'clock, Fargo roused grudgingly to a pounding sound that he first took to be Alice, banging her fist on the headboard.

"Don't be so damned impatient, gal!" he moaned, his eyes still closed. "You're going to wear this man clear out!"

But when he reached for her she wasn't there, and then he realized that some idiot was pounding on his door.

"Hold your damn horses!" he hollered as he struggled into his long johns. He'd pulled his britches on over them and was just buttoning up when the door burst open and two men shouldered their way into the room.

Out of longstanding habit, he reached for his gun, which he'd hung over the bedpost, but stayed his hand when he saw the badges glinting on the chests of his two uninvited guests.

"You Skye Fargo?" said the one wearing the sheriff's badge. Though not much taller than five foot nine in his boots, he was beefy, and looked as though he could have knocked down doors all day and never felt so much as a twinge.

Fargo picked up his shirt and shrugged into it. "You gents make quite an entrance," he said, and flicked his eyes toward the splintered wood. "You're gonna pay for that, I hope. Cause *I'm* not."

The deputy, as tall and lanky as the sheriff was short and wide, stepped forward and looked Fargo up and down with a wary eye. "It's him, Farley. Blond Alice said so. He's the one."

Fargo sat down on the bed and proceeded to pull on his boots. If these boys were coming to a point, he wished they'd hurry up with the whittling. He found he'd worked up quite an appetite the night before. Steak and eggs sounded like it'd fit the bill.

"Alice?" he said, stomping the final booted foot on the floor. His toes slid in the last half inch, and he stood up. "What's this about Blond Alice?"

The deputy drew his gun.

Fargo immediately held his hands out at his sides, palms forward. "Now, whoa up a minute, fellas! I think I've been real hospitable to you, especially seeing as how you busted my door down before I was all the way into my britches. But you go drawing down on me, I'm liable to take exception."

The sheriff rolled a glance at the deputy. "Aw, for Christ's sake, put that away, Simpson. We're all friends here."

The deputy grumbled something under his breath, but holstered his firearm.

Fargo settled his hat on his head, and moved a little closer to his own gun. What was up with these yahoos, anyway? "I think 'friends' might be pushing it just a mite, Sheriff."

"It's Sheriff Tucker," said the thick man. "Farley Tucker."

"All right. Sheriff Tucker, then. As I was saying, my friends generally wait for an invitation before they shove my door off its hinges."

Completely ignoring his speech, Tucker continued. "All we want is to have a little confab with you, Fargo. Nice and friendly. And quit sidlin' toward that firearm."

Fargo's hand halted halfway to it. Again. "And why's that? Seeing as how we're such good friends and all."

Deputy Simpson snarled. "You smart ass son of a—"

Sheriff Tucker elbowed him and he shut up. "Why don't you come on down to the jail, peaceful-like?"

he continued smoothly. "We'll just have us a little conversation. Simpson here has got the coffeepot on."

If the sheriff thought Fargo was going to walk down to the jail for coffee like a calf after the teat, he was sadly mistaken.

"Oh, I don't think so," he said. "This room's as good for talking as anyplace." His Henry was across the room, but in a pinch, he could always pull the Arkansas toothpick from his boot. The two men had been so busy watching his face—and watching the Colt slung over the bedpost—that he doubted they'd noticed the knife or its scabbard.

In fact, both of them looked more than a little nervous, and that deputy, especially, looked like he was about to go off half-cocked. Fargo had a feeling that Tucker was the one to watch, though.

"Where were you yesterday afternoon, Fargo?" the sheriff asked. "Assumin' you are Fargo, that is."

"I am. And I was on my way into town. Rode in from out by Four Tanks. Had a letter to mail for a friend."

The deputy snorted. "That's a three-day ride, and there's no water. You expect us to believe you carried three days' worth of water with no packhorse? You expect us to believe you came straight here?"

"Never said I did," Fargo replied levelly. "I picked up water over by the Flathead range, and I stopped yesterday morning, out by—" He paused. Maybe the McBride brothers didn't exactly want anybody to know they were out there. After all, they'd surely taken a shot or two at him.

"Out there by that spring, about ten or twelve miles west of town," he said. "The one with the big boulders all around, and that thick grove of paloverde and mesquite."

Sheriff Tucker nodded thoughtfully, but his deputy looked like his clothes were full of ants, and they'd just gone on the march.

"Why?" Fargo asked.

The sheriff said, "You see anybody out there? Any Injuns? White men?"

"No, no Indians," Fargo replied. "We done now? I'd like to get some breakfast."

Tucker said, "Oh, I think you seen somebody all right. I think you seen two old coots out there, camped back in the rocks. I think you backshot the both of them and robbed them, and then you turned their mules free. And then you came on into town purty as you please and availed yourself of one of our whores for the night. And I think that today you were gonna ride right on out. Probably whistlin'. You're the coolest son of a bitch I ever saw, Fargo, no doubt about it. Cuff him, Josh. I'll search his belongins."

Before the deputy could take a step forward, Fargo leapt for his gunbelt and smacked Deputy Josh Simpson across the face with it, leaving behind a long red mark where the buckle caught him.

Before the deputy could cry "My eye! My eye!" Fargo lit into the sheriff. A punch to his gut made no dent whatsoever, but when Tucker hauled off and slugged him back, Fargo surely felt it.

Cursing under his breath, Fargo stumbled backward a step, then bent over and charged, ramming his body headfirst into the sheriff's midsection, just as hard as he could.

Tucker doubled over, the wind knocked out of him, and Fargo cracked a vase over his head. Tucker went down in a shower of broken crockery and wilted wildflowers.

The deputy was on his knees and caterwauling about his eye, and Fargo took advantage of the situation to whack him over the skull with the butt of his still-holstered gun.

He, too, crumpled.

Grumbling to himself, Fargo quickly buckled his gunbelt around his waist, then grabbed his Henry and his pack. He had to hotfoot it to the livery and get the Ovaro out of hock. Then he was going back to the McBrides' claim.

The sheriff hadn't said one word about the McBrides' mine, the entrance to which was in full view of their campsite, the place they had supposedly been murdered.

Why not?

Furthermore, nobody had mentioned Clementine.

He slung his legs over the windowsill, skittered down to the edge of the roof, jumped to the ground, and set off at a quick jog for the livery.

And as he approached the stables, he also reminded himself that the next time September Downy asked him to mail a letter, to tell him to go take a hike.

# 3

He rode the Ovaro hard most of the way out to the McBrides' mine, so instead of three hours and a mite, it took him less than two. He walked the Ovaro the last half mile, though. It would cool the horse down.

Besides, he didn't want any plumes of dust giving him away in case somebody was at the mine who shouldn't be.

But when he reached the camp, it seemed deserted. He could find neither Tell nor Tyrone McBride, so he assumed their bodies had been hauled back to town.

The campsite was a mess. The firewood was scattered, and there were signs of scuffle. He kicked aside a stray bedroll, and stepped over a plate that had once been piled with beans and bacon, but now buzzed with flies.

There was no sign of Clementine.

He left the Ovaro to graze beside the spring—along with a single mule that had wandered back—and found a lantern. He lit it, and stepped into the mouth of the mine.

He proceeded cautiously. The McBrides had both been short of stature, and the shaft probably would have given the taller of the two men an inch or so of spare room. Fargo, however, had to crouch.

He worked his way forward, squinted eyes searching the far corners of the lantern's cast yellow glow for any sign of Clementine.

The tunnel sloped gently downward for about twenty feet before it split into a T. He hadn't realized the McBrides had dug so extensively. There was no pile of debris out front—or anywhere else, for that matter—to indicate anywhere near that much activity, and he saw no rails for the ore cart. Of course, he hadn't seen an ore cart, either. Odd. A digging of this size would have produced a sizable rock pile.

Fargo looked to the left, then to the right. Now, which direction?

On instinct, he decided on the left-hand shaft, and had proceeded not more than ten feet along its narrow, rough walls when he heard a scuffling sound behind him.

He wheeled just in time to catch a glimpse of Clementine, swinging a pick at his head with all her might.

He woke to find his head in Clementine's lap and a cool compress being applied to his head.

"I'm so sorry, Mr. Fargo," she was saying. "I thought you were . . . them. I thought they'd come back. Can you speak? Can you hear me?"

He tried to struggle up to a sitting position, but she pressed him back. "Stay put for a little," she soothed. She didn't have to ask twice.

"Was . . . was I out all day?" he croaked. Darkness surrounded them. Even the stars hadn't come out, and the only light flickered feebly from his lantern.

"No, just fifteen or twenty minutes, that's all," she said. "I'm so terribly sorry! If you hadn't ducked I would have . . . I would have . . ." She sniffed, and a tear splattered on Fargo's nose. "As it was, I only hit you with the handle. Thank God. How does your head feel?"

Actually, it hurt like a ring-tailed son of a bitch, but he muttered, "It's all right," and tried to sit up again. Clementine's lap was all well and good, but he had to figure out where he was.

This time he sat up successfully, and put a hand behind him, thinking to steady himself on the wall of the shaft. But there was nothing there, just more of the same rough rock floor upon which he was seated.

"Sure dug it wide," he said under his breath.

"Oh, we're not in the shafts," Clementine said. She got to her feet, and the lantern light washed up her trouser legs. "We're in the cathedral room."

*Cathedral room?*

She stepped away, and then he couldn't see her, only hear her. He now recognized a soft background sound as water: water dripping, then water being scooped up into a container. And then she was back at his side, offering him a tin cup.

"Drink this," she said, pressing it to his lips.

It was water, all right, pure and cool, and he drank it all down. "Where'd you say we were, again? I could have sworn you said 'cathedral.' " He set the cup aside and rubbed at the back of his skull. His fingers met a good-sized lump, and he scowled. "That pick you laid up alongside my head must have shaken my brains loose."

"You heard me right," she said. But instead of answering his question, she asked, "Why'd you come back?"

All right, she was crazy. He could live with a little crazy, he supposed, so long as it was in such a all-fired gorgeous package.

"Because Sheriff Tucker was about to take me to jail for killing your father and your uncle," he said. Perhaps he was too blunt, because she promptly put her hands to her face and burst into tears.

"You *did* do it!" she said between sobs.

"No, Clementine," he said quickly, before she could think to look for something new to hit him with, although where she'd find it in all this endless gloom was a mystery to him.

"I didn't," he continued. "I rode into town and

mailed old September's letter for him, and spent the night at the Palace Hotel. Then, first thing this morning, the sheriff and his deputy broke down my door and started accusing me of murder."

Her fingers parted to reveal one teary, glistening eye. "You swear?"

He nodded. "I swear." He didn't suppose there was much use in telling her not to cry, so he simply put his arm around her shoulders. "What happened here yesterday, after I rode out?"

She sniffed. "I don't know, not really. Daddy sent me down to the ore room to fill another bag, and then I heard someone shooting."

"The ore room?" he interrupted. She was loco, all right. Beautiful, but balmy.

She nodded. "I came running up the shaft, but then I heard men's voices. They were strangers. I just—" She fished a handkerchief out of her pocket and honked her nose in a most unladylike fashion. "I just froze. That was it, pure and simple. Something about the way they were talking . . . I knew Daddy and Uncle Tyrone were dead."

He gave her a little squeeze. "What were they saying, Clementine?"

"I couldn't make out but a snatch here and there. But they were dragging the . . . dragging the . . . bodies . . ." She burst into another torrent of tears, and Fargo held her until they subsided enough that she could continue.

Apparently, she'd heard two, possibly three men, and they were in a hurry.

And she'd heard a name.

"Clay," she said. "I heard one of them call another 'Clay.' But that was all."

Fargo helped her to her feet. "Well, what's done is done." He searched the darkness, trying to find anything to give him his bearings. "The first thing we have to do is get you out of here, to someplace safe."

**17**

It was the first time either of them had spoken above a whisper, and at the echo that spat his words back, over and over, his first inclination was to clap his hands over his ears.

"Shh," Clementine hissed, too late. "You'll bring the whole place down on our heads!"

"*What* whole place?" he whispered.

"I told you," she muttered in disgust. "We're in the cathedral room. Oh, shoot. Here, let me turn a lantern up."

She ducked out of sight—which was fairly easy, all things considered—then came back into view with another lantern, bigger than the one he'd carried into the mine. She lit it, then turned up the wick.

"Jesus!" Fargo breathed.

"Or somebody like him," Clementine concurred.

They were standing in a mammoth cave. The walls were lost in darkness and he had no way of knowing the breadth of the place, but overhead, rafts of pale, creamy stalactites hung down. Below, someone—probably the McBrides—had cleared fallen and broken stone spires from the section of the floor where the two now sat. It looked like a path led away from them, out of the circle, but he couldn't see where it headed.

Right down the center of the cave was what looked like a long, black pool. Fargo took the lantern from Clementine. Boots skidding on the rock, he peered closer.

He saw that it was not really a pool, but an underground river that surfaced here through some oddity of geology. The water was clear and slow moving, not stagnant as he would have expected. He couldn't see any fish in it, although he did spy a few small, shrimplike creatures.

Behind him, Clementine whispered, "It's what feeds the spring out front, Daddy said." And then she began to cry again.

Fargo circled her shoulder with his arm again.

"C'mon, honey," he said kindly. "Show me the way out of here. I've got to get my horse out of sight while I decide what to do."

Fifteen minutes later, the Ovaro—along with the one mule that had come back—was wearing a very peculiar padded hat as Fargo led him down the mine shaft, following along behind Clementine and the mule in the wake of her lantern light.

"Watch his head," she whispered back to him for perhaps the third time.

She didn't have to. He knew all too well that it didn't take much of a blow to the head to kill a horse—particularly if it was struck in the right place—and he was taking extra precautions to keep the Ovaro calm. Nice of the McBride brothers to have thought up these hats, even if they did look pretty stupid.

She led him back the way they'd come, down the right-hand shaft, then right again, then left, until they were in her cathedral room.

"Where are we going?" he hissed. He knew that one overzealous snort or nicker from either the mule or the Ovaro might bring the precarious roof above crashing down on them.

"Just keep following," she whispered back. "And don't let him whinny!"

He followed her along the sheeted rock bank of the river, around piles of broken stone. The echoes of the horses' hooves were magnified tenfold, and he could have sworn he heard a rumbling all around him. He was just about to turn the Ovaro around and take his chances in the broad daylight when she said, "In here."

And then he could see a wall ahead, and a passage opening into it. She led the mule inside, and he followed.

They entered another shaft, but this one was carved by nature, not by miners with picks or dynamite. The ceiling was higher here, and the passage wider and narrower by turns, and there was no danger of the Ovaro cracking his head. In fact, in places the tall horse could have reared and struck nothing but air with his head and hooves.

"We're here," Clementine said in a nearly normal tone of voice. "This is the stable."

He followed her out into a strange sort of rock room, perhaps twenty feet by thirty-five, and dirty from the detritus of centuries. A thin, dusty beam of sunlight filtered down from a hole in the ceiling, which was roughly fifty feet above.

He saw then that iron tie-rings had been hammered into the rock here and there, and he led the Ovaro over to one of them. It was crusted in flaking rust, and all but the inner core of it fell apart in his hands.

"These have been here a long time," he said.

"Spanish," Clementine answered matter-of-factly. She was tying her mule to a similar ring. "Don't know that they'd actually hold up to a good tug, but at least the mule—and your horse—will *think* they're tied." She gestured with her shoulder. "There are oats and hay behind you."

He stripped the tack from the Ovaro, then found the hay and the oats. "Remind me to ask you," he muttered, "just what the hell is going on here."

"Over coffee," she said.

# 4

"So, the Spanish found this place first?" Fargo said. He'd been listening to Clementine talk for about the past hour, and was at the moment seated just inside the mouth of the mine shaft, eating a plate of soupy ham and beans, watching and listening for sounds in the distance.

"They were the ones who dug the shafts," she said. "Coffee?" She held out the pot.

He nodded and she filled his cup.

"They probably just stumbled on it, the same as Daddy and Uncle Tyrone," she added pensively.

"Fell into the stable room, huh?" he said. She'd told him the story, how her father had fallen into a hole in the ground and broken his leg, and Tyrone had lowered himself in after. Tyrone had discovered the other rooms and the mine shafts that connected them. And then he found the silver.

She nodded. "I suppose we'll never know what drove the Spanish out, or what made them leave so much ore behind. But Daddy guessed the Apaches had something to do with it."

It was Fargo's turn to nod. He had to repeatedly remind himself not to stare at her chest. One of the top buttons on her shirt had come undone—while she was dragging him to the "cathedral," he supposed— and he kept catching tantalizing glimpses of the deep shadow between her breasts.

"Anyway," she continued, "Daddy and Uncle Tyrone never laid their claim to it. They thought if anybody knew, they'd be overrun with claim jumpers. That was Uncle Tyrone's doing, I guess. He always was secretive."

Fargo took a sip of his coffee. "Well, eventually they were going to have to let somebody know. They'd have to sell the ore someplace, and according to what I saw down in that 'ore room' of theirs, they were going to need a whole lot of wagons. Not to mention mule teams."

She furrowed her brow. "Naturally," she said, as if he were the class dolt. "But they were going to wait until they'd pretty much mined it dry. It was safer that way. And they had—"

"Wait a minute," he cut in. "I didn't see any signs of mining activity. How long had they been here, anyway?"

She took an exasperated breath. "Daddy broke his leg about four months back, so they hadn't started yet. There was Daddy to heal, and Uncle Tyrone couldn't do much by himself. Uncle Tyrone hid the shaft again, then took Daddy down to Mojave Springs, and they sent for me. The three of us came back out here about ten or twelve days ago, all right?"

Fargo made himself look away from her cleavage. Again. He said, "Just asking."

"Anyway . . . Where was I?"

"They were going to mine it dry," he said.

She nodded. "Yes. There was lots of room to store the ore until they'd finished, and then it would be my turn. Besides cooking and doing odd jobs, I was supposed to hire the wagons and drivers."

"How?" he asked.

"I have some money set by," she said, staring at her boots. "Not a fortune, but enough to put together an ore train." She looked up. "It was the least I could do for my father."

Fargo studied her. Now, how in the world could an old rock breaker like Tell McBride afford to send a daughter all the way back to Boston to school? And how could she manage to scrape together the cash to put together a train of ore wagons? The whole thing smelled fishy to him.

He didn't want to ask right out, so he decided to try the back door. "You mother was from Boston, was she?"

Clementine sat up straight. "Boston? Who said anything about Boston?"

"Your uncle Tyrone," Fargo said. "Yesterday afternoon."

She relaxed, her slim shoulders slouching down once again. "Oh. No, she wasn't. She was from Kentucky. Daddy's people were from Ohio, originally." She nodded, indicating Fargo's plate. "You done with that?"

He was, having scraped it clean, and handed it to her. "You're a good cook."

She shrugged. "A cook's only as good as the fixings."

"So why Boston?" he asked.

Her back was turned to him, but he thought he saw her hesitate. "Why not?" she said.

"Just curious, that's all. You been back there all this time?"

She turned toward him, and her mouth was crooked up in annoyance. "All this time? Just how old do you think I am, anyhow?"

He laughed. "I didn't mean to make it sound—"

She waved a hand, and her face relaxed into a smile. "Sorry. It's been a pretty rotten couple of days for me. I mean, I don't even know where they took the . . . the bodies. I would've liked to have a fancy funeral. Daddy and Uncle Tyrone would have liked that." She sat down. "No, they would've liked to live about twenty years longer . . ."

She began to weep softly again, and Fargo felt help-

23

less. He never knew what to say to a crying woman. It always came out wrong, somehow. So he simply went to her and put his arms around her and let her sob.

At last she stopped, and by then the sun was heading down beneath the horizon.

"Sorry," she said, and politely moved away. She blew her nose into her handkerchief again, and wiped her eyes. "Forgive me. I didn't mean to cry all over you. It seems that's all I do. I'm sure a man like Skye Fargo has better things to do that hang around a weepy woman."

He chuckled in spite of himself. "Wish you wouldn't say 'a man like Skye Fargo,' " he said. "Makes me feel like a bronze statue in a park somewhere. If you don't watch out, you're going to have me ducking imaginary pigeons."

She smiled a little. Even with her nose red and her eyes puffy from all the tears, she was still beautiful. What kind of job had she had back in Boston, anyhow? It seemed to him that if she were out in the public view for any length of time—say, five minutes—some Dapper Dan would have slipped a ring on her finger faster than you could say "How do."

Perhaps she'd worked away from the public eye. A seamstress, possibly, or perhaps a governess or a schoolteacher, maybe in one of those private schools. But still . . .

"Mr. Fargo?"

He remembered himself. "Sorry. Woolgathering, I guess. What did you say?"

"Nothing. Just stop staring at my chest."

He felt himself turn beet red beneath his beard, but before he could offer up an apology, she handed him a stack of plates.

"Come down to the spring and help wash up these dinner things, Mr. Fargo," she said. "Around here, everybody helps clean up, not just the womenfolk. That's a rule."

Schoolteacher. That had to be it.

It was after nine, and they had made up their pallets in the cathedral room, although just barely. Clementine had insisted they camp quite close to the mouth of one of the two shafts coming into the room, in case Fargo snored.

Fargo didn't, but had gone along with it anyway. With his head aimed down the mineshaft, he'd be better able to hear anyone coming. Besides, he didn't relish the idea of trying to sleep with one those huge stalactites, twenty or thirty feet above, aimed at his belly.

Clementine had lit one lantern, which was turned down low and sat between them, illuminating little more than her face and shoulders.

"I think," he said, "that the best bet is for you to go into town tomorrow."

She gave a little snort. Beneath the blanket, her bosom shook with it. She stared up at the ceiling and said, "And do what?"

"Nose around," he said. "After all, you told me you'd never been into town. You said you came out by way of Mojave Springs. Nobody knows you. You can say you're a schoolteacher, looking for work."

She rolled her eyes. "And no one will think it odd if I come riding into town on a mule—bareback, no less—and wearing these clothes? You'll have to do better than that, Mr. Fargo."

She had a point.

"All right," he said. "You can say that you're a widow. That you lost your husband to renegades. That you had to ride the mule because it was the only mount they didn't kill, and you couldn't ride in skirts. That's believable."

She seemed to study on this. "And where did these

renegades attack us? And renegade *what*? Indians? White men?"

Fargo thought. There'd been news of attacks to the southeast. Not for some time—they'd been quiet for over a month, now—but recently enough that she'd more than likely be believed.

"Renegade whites. You can say that you were up in the White Mountains when they rode down on you, and your husband hid you."

"Where?"

Fargo ground his teeth. "I don't know. In the bushes." She was making this complicated. He tried to remember what little news he had heard. "Say that there were five of them, painted up like Indians, and that one wore a lynx hat. They'll believe that. There is such a gang operating southeast of here."

She was silent for a moment, and then she said, "All right. That's better. At least it has something of a ring of truth to it." She turned toward him. "Mr. Fargo, I—"

"Do me a favor, Clementine?" he said, cutting her off.

"Certainly. What?"

"Stop calling me Mr. Fargo, all right?"

She smiled. "Then what shall I call you?"

"Skye. Or Fargo. Anything but *Mister* Fargo," he said grumpily. "Sets my teeth on edge, especially when it comes from a pretty woman."

"Thank you," she said simply. "And I think I'll call you Fargo, if you don't mind. It sounds . . . strong. The way you look."

He felt the flush color his face for the second time that day. This little gal knew just how to get to him, and he didn't know whether to be pleased or annoyed.

He decided to change the subject. "So, did you teach school back East?"

"No."

"Governess?"

"No."

What else could she have done? It wasn't like there were a lot of avenues open for eager but well-schooled young ladies.

He tried again. "Shop clerk? Waitress? Dressmaker?"

"Heavens, no!" she said, and then she chuckled.

"All right," he said with a sigh. "I give up."

She came out of her bedroll, and crawled the few feet between them. Angled across the space, her head near his chest, her bosoms pressing against her shirt, she said, "You promise you'll still help me? That you won't just climb on your horse and ride out of here, never to be seen again?"

He blinked. What could she have done that was so awful she thought he wouldn't help her?

"My God, Clementine," he said. "What did you do? Kill somebody? That's an event, not a job."

She shook her head, smiling wryly. "No, Fargo. I've never spilled anybody's blood. I've never made a dress or a hat, either, nor waited tables, nor educated anybody. Well, not the young, anyhow." Her eyes twinkled.

Fargo waited.

"I was," she said, pulling herself closer, "the mistress of J. Robert Sykes the Third."

"What?" thundered Fargo, and she clapped a hand over his mouth until the echoes died down. J. Robert Sykes, scion of a wealthy family of shipbuilders, had been well-known for his parties and his money and his excesses, even out here in the West. The bigger newspapers carried regular stories of his exploits, both in the shipyards and out of them—the yachts, the weekend foxhunts, the huge galas, the glittering waste of it—and had also carried his obituary. Intoxicated, he had fallen overboard one weekend the previous spring, and was drowned at the tender age of thirty-two.

And the name of the ship from which J. Robert Sykes had taken his nosedive, if Fargo wasn't mistaken, had been . . .

Good grief.

Fargo pulled Clementine's hand away from his mouth. "The *Clementine*? The yacht he fell off of? That was you?"

She shrugged, with a tip of her head. "Well, not me, exactly. Named for me, I guess. And you don't have to be so crass about it. Bobby was a lovely man."

Fargo hissed air through his teeth. "Well, I'll be a cross-eyed son of a bitch. Honey, you're a long way from Boston."

"A long way from everything," she said, and reached to stroke his cheek. "Fargo? Make me feel better."

# 5

"Clementine," he said as she slid closer, until her body was against his, with only the blanket and their clothes between, "you sure are a bag of tricks."

She kissed him lightly along his jawline. "Poor choice of words, Fargo." She pulled away the blanket and began to unbutton his shirt. "Try rephrasing."

"You said J. Robert Sykes?" he said with some difficulty, since she was nibbling on his chest by this time, and one of her hands had slid down under his blanket to rub his already stiffening rod through the fabric of his pants.

"That's right." She had worked her way down his belly to his belt buckle.

"The rich one?"

Her hand left his crotch just long enough to slip free his buckle and unbutton his britches. "There was only the one that I know about," she said, and then her hand, cool and soft, wrapped around his manhood. "Fargo," she said, grinning up at him, "you're all man."

He grinned back. "What did you expect?"

She shrugged. "I've been thinking about you since yesterday afternoon." She gave him a gentle squeeze, and he took a quick breath. She knew what she was doing, all right. "I mean," she continued, "give or take a major tragedy or two. Figured you had a couple of extra pairs of your socks in here. I'm delighted to see that I was mistaken."

"Come back up here," he said, deciding to forget J. Robert Sykes for the time being. "I want to make sure you're not hoarding socks, either."

She chuckled, low and throaty, but instead of sliding up to his face, she sat up in the lamplight. "Goodness," she said, staring at his crotch. "It looks even bigger, now that I have some perspective on it."

She gave him a wicked grin as, slowly, she unbuttoned her shirt, and then she parted it. In the lamplight, her breasts seemed perfect and golden, their undersides heavy and full, her pale pink nipples large, high, and puckered.

"No socks here," she said. She shrugged it off and it fell, leaving her nude to the waist. "But maybe I should show you that I'm entirely sock-free," she said thoughtfully, and with one graceful movement, she rose and stood above him.

Fingers worked deftly at her belt, and he watched as she shucked out of her men's britches, then pulled the tie free from her hair and shook out her lustrous mane. Without a word, she turned slowly so that he could see every inch.

She was gorgeous, no doubt about it. Rich men would have paid thousands for just a single night with her. At least, one had—if her story was true. Long, glistening, gently waving black hair fell over her shoulders and down her back, brushing her waist. Those beautiful breasts were the crowning point of a body that most men would kill for, and that most women would probably die to have.

A narrow waist flared out to round female hips and a triangular thatch of the darkest black curls; and when she turned for him, Fargo admired her round, dimpled buttocks. Her hips tapered into long, strong thighs, graceful calves, and well-turned ankles.

But he wasn't looking at her legs for long.

"Get down here," he said thickly, and throwing aside his blanket, kicked clear of his britches.

"Just think, Fargo," she said, molding her body to his. "You could have been spending the night in jail. And I could have been spending another night cold and alone and scared to death. Isn't it nice how things worked out?"

He took her face in both hands. "Clementine?" he whispered. Her nipples were so hard that he could feel them pressing into his chest.

"Yes, Fargo?"

"Shut up," he said, and then he kissed her.

Her body was lush to the touch as well as to the eye, her flesh firm, her muscles lithe. He rolled her on her back and crouched between her splayed legs, filling his hands with her breasts, then stroking her hips, then her inner thighs.

He dipped his fingers inside her. Her hips rose to meet his hand, forcing his fingers deeper. "Not yet, Clementine," he whispered, and began to rub her gently, his thumb where it would bring her the most pleasure, his fingers slowly moving in and out. He wanted to watch her, to see her body writhe.

Just the sight of her was enough to keep him rock-hard. She was the sort of woman a man wanted to keep naked twenty-four hours a day.

She gyrated under his touch, first moaning, "Now, Fargo, hurry," and then, "Please, oh Skye, please!" and at last he slid her fanny up along his thighs, and buried himself inside her.

He'd worked her to such a pitch that it didn't take long for her to climax, but he couldn't ease up for her now. As she shook and shivered, he took hold of her buttocks and stood on his knees, bringing her with him, and began to thrust into her with long, deep, hard strokes.

She had recovered by then, and she started to help him, bracing herself on her elbows and her feet, rocking with him, her eyes closed and her neck craned back with passion, her mouth gaping and her torso glistening with sweat.

And then she shuddered again, nearly convulsed, and it took him over the edge, too. He pounded into her one last, thunderous time, sending his pole deep, and then he collapsed, still inside her.

They lay there for what seemed a long time, both panting and slick and sated, her inner muscles pulsing around him, gently squeezing him with involuntary contractions.

She spoke first. "Well," she whispered in his ear, "I can see why you're famous, Fargo."

He laughed, and then he kissed her and rolled off, throwing his arm around her on the narrow blanket. She reached across him and down, laying a gentle hand on his shaft. "Good boy," she said to it.

Even now, he stiffened slightly at her touch. He smiled, and began to toy with one of her pale pink nipples. It beaded immediately, a deep rose hue in its hard and swollen center. He pinched it. She made a cooing sound and turned her head to nibble his ear.

"I like you, Fargo," she whispered. "You take my mind off everything but you."

"That's a good thing, is it?"

"Yes," she said, and sat up. Her back to him, she said, "You thirsty?" And before he had a chance to answer, she was on her feet and had moved out of the lamplight.

She was the damnedest woman!

Sheriff Farley Tucker thumped his thumbnail against the lantern on his desk, then looked up at his deputies again. "Damn it," he spat. "I reckon he's got clean away, then."

Josh Simpson, the deputy who had gone with him to arrest Fargo, shook his head. "I can try again, Farley," he said with determination. "I'll try goin' east this time. I seen the tail end of that spotted horse, and his tracks were clear as paint for a good mile going south, but then they just up and disappeared! I mean, he couldn't've just flew away!" He paused. "Could he?"

"No, he couldn't," Tucker said.

Josh was a dolt, all right, and keen on proving it. Farley Tucker once again congratulated himself on cutting young Josh out of this particular deal.

He said, "Josh, he's gone. Man rides a horse like that, why, he could be in New Mexico by morning, I reckon. No," he added, opening a desk drawer and bringing out a sheet of paper, "I'll just send a letter up to Prescott and another down to Tucson, let them know what happened out here."

Josh opened his mouth to argue, but Tucker said, "That'll be all, Josh. You can go on home, now. It's late, nearly ten." Tucker dipped a pen into the inkwell and poised it over the paper.

Josh stood there a moment, then turned on his heel and without another word let himself out of the office. Tucker cleaned off his pen and put the paper away.

The third man, who had been leaning against the front of the jail's single cell, tipped his hat back with his forefinger and said, "You think he'll let it go?"

"Don't know, Clay," said Tucker. "Who can tell with Josh? He's stubborn as a mule."

"And just about as smart," the other man said with no trace of a smile. Dark and burly, Clay Reeves was a tough man and, Tucker grudgingly admitted, a good one to have on your side. But a sense of humor wasn't something anybody had accused him of having.

Tucker closed the drawer on the letter he would never write, and said, "Maybe one of us should go back out to the mine. Make sure Fargo didn't go back."

"Why would he?"

Tucker shrugged. "Never can tell. I've heard

33

enough stories about him to know that he's a pig-headed son of a bitch. Dangerous, too. Maybe we both better go out and check."

Clay snorted. "Well, I never heard any stories. Far as I'm concerned, Fargo's just another no-account drifter."

*So are you,* Tucker thought, *and a blackmailing one, to boot.* But he just sat back in his chair. "You think you can handle just about anything, don't you?"

The other man's eyes narrowed. "You doubting me, Tucker?"

"No. Just askin'."

"You ought'a know by now that I can. Didn't I save your bacon when the Aztec Kid came gunnin' for you?"

Tucker sighed. Lately, Clay always harkened back to that Aztec Kid incident. "Yes, Clay. You did," he said for probably the thirtieth time. "You saved my butt." Clay never mentioned that he'd seen Tucker backshoot a man five years ago down in Monkey Springs, but the threat was always there, always simmering under the surface.

But now that he thought about it, it was probably a good idea to let Clay go out there alone. Maybe Fargo had taken refuge in the mine. Maybe he'd just kill Clay and get him off the sheriff's back for good. After all, Clay had already done the part he was best at: He'd shot both those old miners in the back.

And if Clay killed Fargo? No matter. Things would still chug along just fine. No, strike that. Better than fine.

"All right," said Sheriff Tucker, with just the right amount of grudging irritation. "You go out there in the morning, then. You know what to do. And while you're out there, why don't you poke around down the shafts? We already know about the one natural cave. There might be more."

"I'll look," Clay replied, "but I can guaran-damn-tee you there ain't no more. I don't know why you didn't just lay claim to it when you found it. We're crazy to be doin' all this for just a finder's fee, Tucker."

The sheriff eased his chair back on two legs, until the back of it hit the wall and he was balanced. He slung a short, beefy leg up on top of the desk. "I already told you why. Because that mine's on Zeb Daggett's range. And I don't think he'd take kindly to me minin' a range owned by the Inca Land and Cattle Company, even if no steer has ever wandered down that far."

Clay lit up the smoke he'd been rolling while Tucker spoke. The paper with which it was rolled was as black as the man's hair and eyes. A picture of the Devil, Tucker thought absently.

Clay gave the sulphur tip a shake, then threw it down. "Aw, old Zeb Daggett don't know which end to put the brand on anymore. He's as crazy as a frog on a stove lid. Don't know why you're so scared of him."

"Not scared," Tucker said between clenched teeth. "Respectful. If you'd known Zeb Daggett in his younger days . . ." Tucker shrugged. Clay was too dense to understand.

"It's his land," he went on. "And if a body was to go in there and take his silver, and if Zeb found out about it, there wouldn't be a single place on this green earth to hide in."

Clay snorted.

Tucker ignored him. "Best to take the finder's fee. Everybody's happy that way, and ten percent of somethin's a whole lot better than a hundred percent of nothin'. Don't forget, Clay, there's a lot of ore down there. At least fifteen wagon loads, already dug by some poor Spanish bastards and left to rot."

Clay drew deeply on his smoke and frowned. "Silver don't rot," he said, and Tucker had to bite his lip to keep from laughing at the poor stupid bastard. Clay might be dumb, but it would take even a dumber man to laugh in his face.

"And you should'a done it right off," Clay continued. "Before those two old rock breakers had a chance to find the place. Never would have had to take care of 'em. And we never would have had that Skye Fargo feller mixed up in it. I swear, Farley, you are one stupid peckerwood. Why'd you have to go accusin' him, anyway? It's not like I can't take care of him," he added, a little too quickly, "but if you'd just waited a day—"

"Because we'd already hauled the bodies in, that's why," Tucker said in disgust. "And because you'd already shot your mouth off about it. And because Fargo was the only stranger to have ridden into this goddamn town for the past three weeks. Would'a looked real odd if I hadn't taken him in. Or at least, tried to."

Clay didn't say anything. He just stood there, smoking and scowling.

"Fine," said Tucker, pulling his leg off the desk. He dropped the chair to all fours with a *thump*. "You go out there tomorrow morning. I can almost guarantee you that you ain't gonna find hide nor hair of him, but fine. Go out. Make sure."

"First thing," said Clay.

The sheriff stood up. "First thing," he replied. He hoped Fargo was out there. He hoped Fargo took Clay Reeves's head off. "I'm goin' home and get some sleep."

# 6

At dawn, Fargo rose to find Clementine outside the mine, packing her mule for the ride into town. How in the hell she'd ever led it past him in that echoing cathedral room was more than he could understand, but he decided to let it go.

"Hold on," he said, leaning a shoulder against the rock. "I've got a better idea."

She turned a glowing face toward him. "Good morning, lazybones. Thought you were going to sleep all day."

She came to him and gave him a languorous kiss that nearly had him ready to take her then and there, but then she stepped back.

"Better," she said, smiling like a cream-filled cat. "Now, what's your idea?"

"Something's been bothering me, Clementine," he said. "Well," he added with a grin, "when you give me a chance to think, that is. I don't think you ought to ride into town. I think you ought to come up north with me."

She cocked her head. "North?"

"To Zeb Daggett's place."

"Daggett?"

She hadn't recognized the name, or at least she gave the impression of not recognizing it. The story she'd fed him about her father and her uncle not filing a claim for fear the town would come down with a case of "silver fever" didn't quite ring true. The cry of "Silver!" was always good news, but it didn't bring a torrent of rabid prospectors quite the same as if you shouted "Gold!"

He didn't know if Clementine was in on the plan— or whether she'd just believed what her daddy told her—but either way, the more he thought about it, this mine was likely on land owned by the Inca Land and Cattle Company. At least, they owned or leased most all the land north, from about here on up into the mountains.

Therefore, the rightful owner was Zeb Daggett. If he was still alive. Daggett would have to be about seventy by now, and Fargo hadn't seen him for four years, not since that blowup on the Mogollon Rim back in '56.

"Fargo?" she asked. "Who on earth is Zeb Daggett?"

"Let me get my horse," he said.

A half hour later, the Ovaro was outside and tacked up, and they set out toward the north.

"I don't like people who keep secrets, Fargo," she said as they jogged along. She was getting peevish by this time, and he supposed he should tell her. But how? If she'd been led to believe that she was about to become very wealthy, it was going to be quite a blow. On the other hand, if she already knew the silver didn't belong to her, she might just take off.

Not that the mule she was riding would be any match for the Ovaro, of course. But it would be hard traveling for a day with a woman who didn't want to travel.

Well, what the hell.

"Clementine," he said, readying himself to grab for her reins, "Zeb Daggett owns the Inca Land and Cattle Company."

She hiked a brow. "So?"

"The Inca Land and Cattle Company owns or leases about ten thousand acres, pine to desert."

She gave him an exasperated look. "That's nice for Mr. Daggett, but what does it have to do with me?"

He cleared his throat. "We're . . . we're riding on his land right now."

"And?"

She didn't get it. He tried again. "Clementine, there was a reason your father and uncle didn't file a claim on that mine."

"Of course!" she said. "They didn't want to start a . . ." And then her delicate brow creased. Her whole face fell into a look of woe, then twisted into disgust. "Uncle Tyrone again!" she hissed. "I should have known there was something crooked going on! Every time Daddy got around Uncle Tyrone, he—"

"Quiet!" Fargo suddenly spotted a speck of dust to the east that could only be a rider. It was headed not toward them, but toward the mine.

"Come on, Clem," he said, and rode down behind a rise.

"What is it?" she asked.

"Just wait here." He jumped down from the Ovaro, pulled his spyglass from his pack, and crawled to the top of the rise.

Fargo looked and saw one man, and he was in a hurry. And he was headed straight for the old mine.

Fargo watched as he rode into the camp and dismounted. He poked around, going through the packs outside the mine, scattering their contents, and then he stood at the mouth of the mine for several minutes, hands on his hips, just staring into the gaping blackness.

"What's going on, Fargo?" Clementine hissed. She'd crawled up the rise, too, and was on her belly next to him.

"I thought I told you to stay with the mounts," he said with irritation, but when she gave no indication that she had any intention of going back down, he added, "It's a good thing we left when we did."

He lifted the spyglass to his eye again, and saw that the man was turning, as if he were scouting the horizon. Fargo saw something glinting on his chest. A badge.

"Why?" Clementine asked. "What is it?" She made an abortive grab for the spyglass, but he pushed her hands down.

"The law," he said. "And stop that." This was neither Sheriff Tucker nor the deputy he'd had with him yesterday, Josh Simpson. This was a new man entirely.

Fargo watched as the man rooted through the McBride brothers' belongings and came up with a lantern, which he appeared to light. Holding it high, he started back into the mine. Fargo lost sight of him.

Thoughtfully, he collapsed the spyglass and slid it into its leather case. Who was this new man, and why had he ridden all the way out here, and alone?

"Fargo, if you don't start talking real soon, I'm going to—"

"Come on," he said, cutting her off, and slithered down the rise to the horse and mule. She skidded down after him, and when they were both on their feet again and she was busy dusting herself off, he said, "One man, and he was wearing a badge. He was snooping around the mine."

"You think he was looking for you?" Clementine asked, and he found he was pleased that she seemed worried.

"Looking for something," he said. "C'mon, I'll give you a boost."

"Are we going back?" she said from the saddle.

Fargo swung up onto the Ovaro. "No. Going up to Daggett's."

He started north, and Clementine followed. They kept to a walk so as to raise as little dust as possible.

He had a very bad feeling about this yahoo showing

up and taking a stroll down into the shaft like he owned the place. But he couldn't exactly ride down there and demand to know what the tin badge was doing, not without bringing on a confrontation for which he wasn't fully prepared.

He was glad they'd ridden out over the rocks to the west of the mine. There'd be no trail to follow. And since they'd packed up everything Fargo had, and—so far as he knew—everything of Clementine's, there was nothing left to indicate that there had ever been anyone there but the McBride brothers.

Even if the deputy found the silver—and Fargo was pretty sure that was exactly what he was looking for, although for the life of him he couldn't imagine how the deputy had known it existed—he wouldn't be able to haul it out before Fargo brought Zeb Daggett's boys down from the north.

Clementine rode up beside him. "Fargo?"

"Yes, Clementine?"

She looked up at him from beneath beetled brows. "You want to unravel this thing for me now, or do I have to get naked again?"

Despite himself, he laughed. "All right, Clem. But you have to promise to get naked later."

He began, so far as he was able, to explain.


Clementine McBride had been seventeen, going on eighteen, when she graduated from Miss Mortimer's Finishing School for Young Ladies of Good Breeding. Contrary to the school's advertising, Miss Mortimer had never asked about her "breeding," which was just dandy with Clementine. What could a girl say when her father was alternately grub-staking or trapping all over the West—sometimes rich, but mostly poor as a church mouse—and her mother had been a whore in a backwoods Ohio saloon?

Daddy never said a bad word about Mama, though.

He'd taken her away from all that, Clementine supposed. Good for Daddy.

But when she was twelve, the Crows had killed her mama—and would have killed her, if she hadn't been secreted in the cellar under the cabin Daddy had "borrowed" while he was running his string of traps. Soon after, Daddy had sent her back East.

While she was at school and eating up her father's savings, she'd come up with several good stories to veil her past. By the time she graduated, she'd settled on the last one. It was the one she'd told to J. Robert Sykes, but it hadn't even crossed her mind to try to pass it off on Fargo.

Curious.

She admired him as they rode along. She liked the leanness of him, the hardness; the firm, angular planes of his body; the hawk sharpness of his eyes. He wasn't soft, like Bobby had been. She wasn't proud of what she'd been or what she'd done, but the name of the game was survival, wasn't it?

And Fargo was a survivor. Maybe that was why she hadn't felt the need to lie to him. He was a kindred spirit. In his lake blue eyes, there was the look of a man who had seen just about everything at least twice, and had lived to tell about it. Or to keep it under his hat.

She would never have met him if she'd stayed back East. She'd never have been able to spend any time with her father, either.

But then, maybe if she hadn't come, Daddy and Uncle Tyrone wouldn't have gone ahead with this harebrained scheme of theirs. After all, it was only when she wired him that she had some money put away that he'd sent for her.

She found she was crying silently, and wiped away a tear.

Damn that Bobby, falling off his own boat in the middle of Boston Harbor in the dark, hard center of

the night! Damn him for not making a will, and damn
him for never having learned to swim; and especially,
damn him for drowning and leaving her exactly
nowhere.

He'd been a drunken fool all his life—a sweet one,
but a drunken fool nonetheless. And in the space of
the first sixteen hours after his death, his mother's
lawyer had shown up and thrown her out of Bobby's
house and onto the street, and stood over her the
whole time she was packing to make certain she didn't
steal anything!

Well, she did manage to get away with that dia-
mond stickpin. . . .

But after dithering for a few months, she'd received
the wire from her father, and she'd come West. But
now her father was dead, and everything she owned—
aside from a dwindling bank account in Boston—was
packed behind her on this stupid mule, and she was
going who-knew-where to tell a man she'd never met
that she'd found his goddamn silver, mined for him
three-hundred-odd years ago by some unknown Spaniards, and wouldn't he like to come pick it up?

"Jesus," she muttered under her breath. "I am an
idiot."

Fargo twisted toward her, the fringe on his buckskins swinging slightly, and frowned with concern. He
dug a handkerchief out of his pocket and handed it
to her.

"It'll be all right," he said.

She must have looked at him oddly, because he
flushed and scowled.

"Hell," he grumbled. "I never know what to say to
a crying woman, anyway."

She gave him the best smile she had in her at the
moment. It was weak, but it worked. She said,
"You're doing fine, Fargo." She blew her nose, then
tucked his handkerchief into her pocket until she

could wash it for him. "How much farther is it, anyway?"

"A good piece," he replied. "Up in the mountains." He pointed ahead, to the distant peaks, misty and blue-green. "By dark, I reckon, if we push and if luck's with us. Walking to keep the dust down has slowed us up a bit, though. We might have to make camp."

Despite everything, a shiver raced up her spine at the thought of spending another night with him, this one under desert skies. Or mountain skies. She had no idea of distance out here. But she found she needed him, needed his strong arms around her, needed him to make the world go away if only for a little while.

"Whatever you say, Fargo," she said quietly. "Whatever you say."

# 7

Clay Reeves set his lantern down outside the mouth of the mine, then squatted beside it, rocking from heel to toe.

He'd already known about the silver ore piled back in there, falling out of ancient, rotting burlap sacks. There was literally tons of it, a pile as tall as he was and maybe twenty feet around. Some of it was so pure that there was almost no need to smelter it. And it was just waiting for somebody to stumble across it.

Somebody like him, for instance.

But he hadn't known that if a man turned right instead of left where the shaft came to a T, he could find a cave that made the one with the mined ore look like a terrier next to a draft horse.

And there was more silver. He'd walked along the wall, holding his lantern high, and he'd seen it, streaking through the walls in thick, sooty streaks, some as wide as his hand, black and deep gray through milky quartz.

He pulled the bandanna from around his neck and swiped at his forehead. There was no telling how deep it went, no telling how much silver was back in this hill, sealed in stone, just waiting for somebody to come and dig it out.

He smiled.

Sheriff Tucker didn't know about the other cave. To the best of Clay Reeves's recollection, Farley

Tucker had only been in the mine just once, when they found the silver together and had become grudging partners. So there was only him and those two old coots, and the old coots were presently laid out on slabs at the undertaker's in town.

Smiling absently, he reached over and picked up the lantern, then raised the shade and blew it out. Might as well start conserving fuel now. It was a long way from town, and supplies.

He set the lantern aside, thinking that maybe ol' Farley didn't need to know. Maybe the sheriff could have himself a little accident. Then he could quit deputying and come out here and dig to his heart's content, with nobody to bother him until the ore was all dug out.

"No," he muttered to the paloverdes and the rocks. "That'll take too long."

He couldn't blast, not without that big cave falling in on itself. And dear Christ, he didn't even want to think about moving thousands of tons of worthless rock, dirt, and caliche just to get back to the ore again.

No, it'd have to be mined from the inside, and quietly, at that. No good being rich if you were dead and buried under tons of rock.

But it could be done. The old pick marks on the wall, left by those long-dead Spaniards who had made the tunnels, attested to that. They'd probably hauled it straight from the big cave down to the little one. Maybe something could be rigged, something like a tent around where he was working at the moment, to muffle the sound. . . .

Funny how those Spaniards had up and left and abandoned the mine. Not to mention the ore. Maybe the Apaches had run them out.

That was another thing to think about.

He stood up and his knees complained loudly, making sounds like coarse grit in a tumbler. Maybe he'd have to let Tucker in on it after all. He'd need help digging, and he could always get rid of Tucker later, couldn't he?

And as for Fargo, he was long gone. No sign of him. He'd found a broken lantern and an old blanket back in the big cave, the one with the silvered walls. Maybe those old McBride brothers had been using it for a sleeping room, or for a place to throw their trash. That wall didn't look like anybody had been close to it for centuries.

It wouldn't be a good place to sleep, now that he thought of it. If a man so much as snored or let out a good holler in his sleep, he'd run a good chance of bringing the whole place down.

He and Tucker could come out here and mine— maybe in shifts—to their hearts' content. Nobody would be the wiser. Maybe he could convince Tucker to quit and they could both mine it full time. That'd leave that moron Josh Simpson in charge of the town.

He snorted out a laugh.

Still smiling, he walked the short distance to the spring, collected his horse, and stepped up into the saddle. He'd let Tucker help him mine the rock. Hell, maybe he'd even let him pay for the wagons they'd have to lease to move it out of there!

He sat there on his squat bay gelding, staring at the black mouth of the mine, not wanting to leave, yearning to go back down the tunnel to the big cave and look one more time, to make sure the silver was really there.

But instead, he grumbled, "Hell, Reeves. You're gettin' squirrely in your old age. What do you think? That somebody's gonna sneak in and disappear it overnight?"

He started back to town at a jog.

The shadows were growing long, and Fargo knew they weren't going to make it to the Inca Land and Cattle Company's headquarters tonight. The wild country was filled with cougar and bear, and the occasional two-legged predator. He'd think long and hard about traveling through these mountains at night if he were alone, and with Clementine's safety to consider, there was no question of going further. So, for the last fifteen minutes, he'd been scouting for a place to make camp.

"All right, Clem," he said when they rode into an old beaver meadow, thick with grass, that edged the creek they'd been following. "I reckon this is as good a place as any to stop for the night."

The tips of the surrounding pine and juniper glittered bright in the sun, and the trunks were lost to the shadow of late afternoon. A small grove of chokecherry had sprouted up in the center of the clearing, and he reined in the Ovaro beside it. They'd bed down here, beside the chokecherry, and he could hobble Clementine's mule and the Ovaro and let them graze until dark. There was plenty of grass.

She slid off her horse before he did, and wincing, rubbed at her backside.

"About time!" she said, and he held back a smile. He supposed Boston boating parties didn't do much to toughen up a gal's saddle-sitting muscles.

At least she wasn't helpless, not by a long shot. She had the saddle off her mule by the time he dismounted.

"Is it very much farther?" she asked.

He stripped his horse of tack, too. "No. If we get going by dawn, we ought to make it before noon," he replied, leading the animals out into the high grass and hobbling them. They set into grazing immediately. As he got to work stringing up a picket line for later, he noticed that Clementine was already gathering firewood.

They were well up into the mountains. Pine forests that had started out scrubby gradually changed as they climbed higher into a canopy of towering pine and fir, interspersed with the occasional sycamore or juniper or oak. Zeb Daggett had built his empire in the high country, close to the thirty-fifth parallel: a route he was certain the railroads would use, once they got out this far. In the meantime, he sold cattle and horses, pushing them east to New Mexico over the trail blazed by the Army Corps of Topographical Engineers about ten years ago.

To the best of Fargo's knowledge, it wasn't a trip Daggett made every year. It was still very wild country this far west, and regardless of what anybody said, Daggett wasn't crazy. Besides, Daggett only sold off the surplus, always holding back the best of the breeding stock for himself and letting the herds increase while he waited patiently for the railroad.

Zeb Daggett was a man who thought ahead, but perhaps he'd thought a little too far ahead this time. Fargo figured it'd be at least twenty years before those dunderheads back East got around to laying tracks this far to the southwest.

On the other hand, what was bad for Daggett was good for him. He was in no hurry to see civilization creeping into these mountains, laying axes to these towering trees and running the Indians out. Live and let live, he figured.

He joined Clementine in the clearing. She'd already kicked a clear place in the grass and started the fire, and was crouched on one knee, feeding it sticks and twigs.

At his approach, she looked up. "Sorry, I didn't take time to get rocks for a firebreak," she said. "I was in a hurry. I'm starving to death!"

From the creek, Fargo brought stones to ring the fire, and then he brought water for the coffee. He settled back to watch her work. Soon, the scent of coffee was in the air, as well as the salty aromas of bacon sizzling, beans bubbling and skillet bread baking.

"Old J. Robert Sykes teach you how to cook like this?" he asked.

She didn't look up, being occupied with turning the bacon. "The only thing Bobby Sykes could have taught anybody about cooking was how to use room service," she said, one corner of her mouth hitched up into a smile. "Or maybe, how to screw the serving girl." The smile fell.

"Sorry," he said. "Didn't mean to pry."

"It's all right," she said, and sat back away from the fire. "You're not prying. Fact is, my mother taught me campfire cooking before I was twelve. She was the best, bar none." She slid a glance toward Fargo, and she must have seen the question on his face, because she said, "Indians killed her when I was twelve. Crow."

"Sorry."

"You say that a lot."

He smiled. "Sorry."

She laughed.

"You know," he began, "I've always thought that—" and then he stopped, and held up his hand to silence her question.

Birds had suddenly risen, close to the north, and an eerie quietness had fallen over the land. Two riders, possibly three, Fargo intuited. Slowly, he put a hand alongside his holster and drew his Colt.

Motioning Clementine to lie flat, where she'd be hidden by the surrounding grasses, he slowly rose and called toward the pines, "I know you're lurking back in those trees! Come out and be recognized!"

He heard the sounds of hooves swishing through the weeds, then, and before many seconds had passed, shadowy forms approached, and took shape.

"Fargo?" whispered Clementine from the ground.

"Shhh!" he hissed.

The first rider to emerge into the clearing was mounted on a bright red sorrel, and wore upon his head a racoon hat, with the animal's mask at its crown. This was above a long, gray-bearded face and buckskins, much like Fargo wore, except that even from here, he could tell they had a lot more road on them.

The second man rode out directly upon the heels of the first and was just as dirty. He wore a torn felt hat, and his black beard was tamed into dozens of long, thin braids. His horse was more sedate in color, a black bay, and the pack mule he led was loaded down, probably with furs.

"Don't shoot!" said the first rider, and held out his hands to show that they were empty.

"Don't go pluggin' us, mister!" hollered the second one as the two sat their mounts about twenty feet out. "We just smelt your vittles and come down for a look-see!"

He stuck his thumb out toward his companion and said, "This here old coon-hatted graybeard is Lush Fillpot, whose brain's in his gull-durn stomach, and my handle's Weasel Smith. Mighty sorry if we's disturbin' you, mister. Reckon we can make our camp somewheres else."

"But I'm hungry, Weasel!" the first one hissed to the second. "I know he's got coffee and bacon and . . ." He sniffed the air again. "And fresh-made bread, too! I haven't had real bread since—"

"Shut up, Lush," said Weasel, and tipped his hat to Fargo. "Well, beggin' your pardon," he said. "We'll be off." He started to rein his horse around.

They did look pitiful, but Fargo was of a mind to let them go. He sure didn't want to spend what could be his last night with Clementine in the grimy company of Lush Fillpot and Weasel Smith.

But then Clementine tugged at his pants cuff. "Fargo!" she hissed. "They haven't had a decent meal for a dog's age!"

She must have said it a little too loud, because Lush

Fillpot, his forehead creasing in dirty lines, craned his head and said, "Is there somebody else there?"

Weasel lifted his head and sniffed the air, testing it. "By crikey, I think you're on to something, Lush. Hey, you got a female over yonder? Is that female cookin'?"

Both men had gone past woeful, and suddenly looked so forlorn that Fargo took pity on the both of them. If worse came to worse, he supposed he could defend Clementine against a couple of ratty old trappers with mischief on their minds. Better here, where he could keep an eye on them, than out there lurking in the trees.

"Come on in," he shouted, and Clementine sat up to peer over the grass. He saw Lush look at her, then saw his mouth pop open in surprise. "Mind your *p*'s and *q*'s, though, fellas."

Weasel, though, wasn't so easily distracted. Glancing at Clementine, he looked back at Fargo. "You got our names, mister, but I don't believe I heard yours."

"It's Fargo," he said, holstering his pistol. "Skye Fargo. Come help yourself to the chuck. It'll be ready by the time you get your horses seen to."

Weasel Smith hadn't moved. "Skye Fargo, you say?"

He nodded.

"Well, I'll be diddly damned!" Weasel's braided black beard spilt to expose a grin like a picket fence with a few boards missing. "By gum, Lush, we's about to take our evenin' vittles with an honest-to-God legend!"

# 8

"So I says, 'Whoa up, there, Lush, you nearsighted old gopher! That there's a sizzled bear carcass, not Old John Hanks burnt to a crisp! You ever see a man with claws like that?' " Weasel helped himself to the last of the beans. "And that's how a bear near came to be buried right and proper, and with full Christian services."

Fargo watched as Clementine wiped away tears of laughter. All things considered, he was feeling pretty damn lighthearted himself. The pair of old trappers were good company even if you had to keep upwind of them, and even if they had eaten two days' rations in one sitting. He didn't know where the hell they put it all.

Lush picked up the coffeepot and turned it upside down over his cup, to no avail. "Darn," he said, tucking his chin into his scraggly gray beard. Behind the empty eye sockets of the racoon's mask above his eyes, Fargo thought he saw something moving and shuddered involuntarily.

If Lush had lice, they were damn big ones.

Clementine took the coffeepot from him. "No trouble to make more," she said happily, and started for the creek, her backside swishing as she walked off into the dark of a mountain night, lantern swinging in one hand, the coffeepot in the other.

Happening over the trappers had done wonders for

her, at least for the time being. Although he harbored some disappointment—all right, a lot of disappointment—that she wouldn't be sleeping in his bedroll that night, Fargo welcomed anything that took her mind off her father's and uncle's murders, if only for a little while.

Lush Fillpot, he noticed, was watching that backside, too. *You're never too old,* he thought, and grinned.

"Seems you fellas are packing down pelts pretty late in the year," he said to fill the time until Clementine got back. All the stories they'd told had been aimed at her. Well, all the stories Weasel had told, anyway. Lush seemed the introspective type, and focused more on his plate—or the scab on his thumb, or the itch on his elbow—than the outside world.

"Yup," said Weasel. "I reckon we are. We was late gettin' around on account of Lush here busted his dang leg right at the last minute. He were fordin' the creek, and a big ol' log got him."

Fargo twisted his head.

"It were floatin' downstream," Weasel said by way of explanation. "Musta been axed and got away from the fellers what chopped it, that's all I can figure. Anyhow, the dad-blamed thing pinned him smack up against a boulder. Took Old Bess—that's our mule—to pull it off him."

"Lucky you had her," Fargo said. Clementine had come back by that time, and was busily grinding fresh coffee beans.

"You walk very well, all things considered, Mr. Fillpot," Clementine said to Lush. She gave the crank a final turn, then looked up at Weasel. "You must have done a wonderful job setting it."

Beneath the dirt, Weasel blushed. This time, he was the speechless one.

Fargo held back a chuckle. A kind word from a beautiful woman went miles and more with these boys.

He said, "I'm surprised you didn't go up to Daggett's spread to cash out your pelts. Either that, or the trading post."

"Tried," said Lush with a scowl.

"We ain't exactly welcome," added Weasel.

"My goodness," said Clementine, setting the coffee on a rock to heat. "Why on earth not?"

"It was on account of somethin' Lush heared," Weasel said in a low tone.

Clementine leaned toward him. "Something he overheard?" she asked. Fargo could see why she'd done so well in Boston. He didn't imagine there was a man alive she couldn't charm. It was obvious that Weasel was smitten. Lush, too.

"Yes, ma'am," Weasel said, nodding. "See, we was up to Daggett's—just rode in—and we happened to be sittin' outside the front winder—"

"It was me, ma'am," the normally closemouthed Lush piped up. "I was sitting on the porch."

"You wanna tell it?" Weasel snapped.

Lush shrugged his shoulders. "Go ahead," he said. He produced a pocketknife, and began to whittle on a length of pine branch waiting to go in the fire.

"All right, then," Weasel said.

"What was it, Mr. Smith?" Clementine asked softly, although Fargo couldn't imagine that she cared. It was nice of her, though, to show them so much attention.

"It was that dang Farley Tucker, ma'am, he who's taken himself the sheriffin' job down to Jupiter."

Fargo's ears perked up.

"We—that is, Lush—heard him talkin' to Old Man Daggett," Weasel continued. "Seems him and his deputy stumbled across what they claimed was the old Santa Rosa Mine, and smack dab on Daggett's leased land. 'Course, we didn't believe him, not for a minute. That mine's nothin' but a story, and a spooky one at that, something Spanish mamas have been scarin' their kids with for maybe three hundred years."

If Clementine caught on, she gave no sign whatsoever. Fargo decided he wouldn't want to play poker with her. He himself was taken aback that the mine was legendary. He'd thought it was just another forgotten relic of the Spanish exploration.

But Clementine batted her lashes just a tad and said, "Really, Mr. Smith? Do go on! Sheriff Tucker said he found this legendary mine? The Santa Rosa, did you call it?"

"Yes he did and yes, I did, ma'am," said Weasel. "That's just how big a liar that Tucker is. Been a liar all his life. Why, I remember back in '53, when he was up on the Platte and I was panning nearby, he come by my camp and said as how—"

"The mine, Mr. Smith?" Clementine urged gently.

"Oh." Weasel scratched at his head. "Well, Tucker said him and his deputy, that son of a bitchin' Reeves—pardon my swearin', ma'am—had found a spring and were scoutin' around, looking for a feller what robbed a dry-goods store, and they come across it. Said it was hid from view pretty good, and when they went inside they found a cave."

Weasel gave his head a shake, and his beard braids danced. "Criminy, couldn't he think of a better story than that? A cave down a mine shaft!"

"Do tell, Mr. Smith!" Clementine fairly squealed.

Weasel reached for the coffee. "You reckon this pot's ready?"

Both Fargo and Clementine said "Yes!" at the same time.

While Fargo waited on tenterhooks—and he supposed Clementine was doing the same, since she bit her own lip so hard that a tiny spot of blood appeared for an instant before she licked it away—Weasel poured himself a fresh cup, and Lush did the same.

"Anyway," Weasel finally went on, "seems ol' Farley and this deputy found themselves a few tons of mined ore down in that cave, and not just any old mined ore. Said this was past high grade. Said they was some rocks that was near pure silver, with the quartz streaked though it, the way silver's usually streaked through the quartz."

"No fooling," said Fargo.

Weasel made a face. "Bunch'a hog slop, if'n you ask me."

Lush nodded.

"Maybe not," muttered Clementine.

Fargo shot her a guarded look across the campfire.

"Furthermore," said Weasel, who apparently had missed Clementine's comment, "Farley Tucker says to Old Man Daggett that he's real sorry he didn't come up right away and tell him he found the damn thing, but right now they got trouble, because there's a coupla fellers out there who are tryin' to mine it. Farley's afeared that he's not gonna get his finder's fee, y'see?"

He took a gulp of coffee, and this time Clementine remained quiet.

Weasel set his cup aside. "Well, Daggett tells him to run those fellers outta there, he don't care how, and to keep the whole thing under his hat. And Tucker says he don't know that he can control Clay Reeves—that's the deputy—"

Fargo saw Clementine mouth *Clay.*

"—for too awful long," Weasel went on, "and then Lush here sneezes, and the both of 'em stop talkin'." Weasel shook his head. "Old Man Daggett kicked us plumb off his place, and said we wasn't welcome at the tradin' post, neither. Old Man Daggett tells you that you ain't welcome, you'd best be believin' him. So we tarried a few days with them half-breed Injun gals Levi Mankiller's got up to his shack, and then we started down the mountain. End of story. Well, we was goin' down to Jupiter anyhow, sooner or later. Lush has got a boy down there he wants to pass the time with."

"My son," Lush said. "Josh." He went back to his coffee and his whittling.

"He'd be a full-grown man by now, wouldn't he, Lush?" Weasel said. He looked toward Clementine, his head twisting curiously.

Clementine didn't notice. She continued to stare grimly into the fire, and to distract Weasel's attention, Fargo asked, "What's this about a legend, fellas? I thought I'd heard them all, but I don't believe I ever heard one about the Santa Rosa Mines."

Lush looked up from his coffee cup and nodded seriously. Weasel, however, leaned forward. "It's short, but there's juice in it, Fargo. Seems them Spanish fellers was diggin' it back in the fifteen hundreds. Well, maybe sixteen hundreds. A long time ago, anyhow. Found a real rich vein, they say. They dug and they dug, but then, strange things started to happen. Firstly, two fellers turned up dead, and they never figured out what killed 'em. Weren't a mark on 'em, accordin' to the story.

"Then the Apaches started pesterin' 'em pretty bad. Lost a few more men. And then pretty soon most'a the men wouldn't work the mine no more, said they was spirits back in the rocks, spirits that didn't want that silver dug."

Weasel helped himself to another cup of coffee. "They sent riders south to San Xavier, hopin' for more men, and for wagons to get their silver out, 'cept the fellers at the Presidio down there had their hands full with Injun problems of their own. So they never sent nobody," he said with a shrug. "And the fellas that was supposed to be workin' the mine never came back, neither."

"Quite a tale," Fargo said.

"There's more," said Lush.

Weasel nodded. "About sixty year back—back when there weren't nobody out here but the snakes and the buzzards—there were a feller named Lester

Sprout what claimed he found it. Said the mine was all full'a bones and such, Spanish bones, though how he knew to tell is more'n I can say. Anyhow, they say that Lester came out'a that wasteland with a sack of near pure silver over his shoulder. He went back for more, but he never come out again. Reckon that mine ate him up, too. Either that, or the Apache."

Lush set his empty cup down. "Ma'am," he asked meekly, "I'm sorry to bother you, but I've still got some holes that need filling. You suppose you could find us some dessert? If it's not too much trouble, that is. Or some more bacon, maybe?"

Weasel frowned. "Now, Lush, don't go chatterin' away at the lady. If'n she had more, she would'a offered."

Clementine looked up, and her grim countenance was gone. There was no sign on her face of anything besides neighborliness. "I've got some sugar and those fresh berries you gents picked for me. I could bake us up a nice skillet cobbler, if you don't mind waiting."

Lush smiled shyly. "Just what I had in mind, ma'am."

"A pure treat," said Weasel.

She rose to go fetch the sugar, and as she did, Fargo asked, "You boys mind some company on the trail tomorrow?"

Clementine, standing at their backs, stopped and twisted toward Fargo, but held her tongue.

"Don't see why not," Weasel replied.

"We'd be pleased," said Lush.

Clementine's nostrils flared with exasperation, but she turned on her heel and headed for the picket line and their stores, which Fargo had placed up a tree.

# 9

Lush and Weasel had bedded down an hour ago and both had sunk into snoring, a sort of complementary harmonic rumbling that Fargo supposed had grown out of long acquaintance.

In contrast, Clementine was silent. Across the fire, her back was turned toward him, a hard line beneath her blanket.

And then she stirred. She didn't look toward him, didn't look toward anybody at all, just rose up and wandered across the moon-silvered meadow aimlessly. Silently, he threw back his blanket and followed her.

He caught up with her at the tree line. "Clementine?" he said softly, and reached for her shoulder.

She turned toward him, and her face wasn't streaked with tears, as he had half expected, but was instead hardened into the sharp angles of despair.

"Clay," she spat. "I heard one of the men call the other one Clay. Don't you see, Fargo? It was the deputy that killed my daddy and Uncle Tyrone. Maybe the sheriff, too. The same men who tried to pin the murders on you."

"Same sheriff, different deputy," he said.

She snorted. "And what good will it do us to go south again? You know those men are going to be lying in wait for us no matter where we go! The town, the mine . . ." She hugged her shoulders, as if to comfort herself. "There isn't anyplace safe down there, Fargo! Why can't we just get out of here? Go away and pretend nothing happened?"

He reached out to stroke her cheek. "Nothing happened? You're forgetting your father."

She brushed away his hand. "I'm not forgetting him, or Uncle Tyrone, either. Trust me, I'm not forgetting anything. I just don't believe they'd want me to get myself killed over that mine, too. Not to mention you."

Fargo sighed. "All right, Clem. I'll take you up north to the trading post and put you on a stage going east."

She cocked her head. "And what about you?"

He didn't hesitate. "I'm going south."

"Why? To put things right? Who made you the keeper of truth and justice?"

"Nobody. I'm the keeper of my own reputation, though. For all I know, Sheriff Tucker's putting out paper on me right now. It would sort of bother me if that paper were to follow me all over the place. It'd make it hard to get a drink, for one thing, if the law was always doggin' me."

"You'd suffer God-knows-what just for your *reputation*?" she said in amazement.

"You don't have to make it sound like I'm crazy," he said softly, smiling. "Sometimes, a man's reputation is all he has."

She looked away for a moment and seemed to consider this. "A woman's, too, I suppose," she said softly, at last. "And the Lord knows I've got very little of that left . . ."

She finally looked up at him. "All right. For all intents and purposes, my reputation's shot east of the Mississippi. Maybe I can salvage a smidgen of it in the West."

"Clem," he said, "you don't have to come south with me. In fact, I'd rather that you—"

"We'll go south, Fargo," she said, cutting him off.

**61**

"We'll go south, and somehow, we'll prove that those murdering yahoos killed Daddy and Uncle Tyrone. And that Mr. Zeb Daggett put them up to it. He may be rich, but that's nothing to me. I've dealt with the rich, and they back down easy once you hold their feet to the fire."

He raised an eyebrow, and she added, "Metaphorically speaking, of course. And I don't care about the silver," she added. "Let it rot in peace along with those bones Daddy said he buried."

Fargo frowned. "What bones?"

"The bones of those dead Spaniards Mr. Smith was telling us about," she said. "Daddy said when they first found that little cave, there were piles of them, all brittle and falling to dust. He and Uncle Tyrone hauled them out and buried them on the desert."

Fargo shook his head slowly. It was true then, the old legend. "I'll be damned."

"Fargo?"

"Yes?"

"Make love to me," she said, drawing closer. "Make love to me right now, right here." Her hands splayed across his chest, plucked at the buckskin, played with the fringe. "Help me make a fresh start."

He rested his hands on her shoulders, running his big thumbs under her shirt, along her collarbones. "A fresh start?"

"Because I'm making a pact with you, Fargo," she murmured. "I'm making a pact right here and now. If you're the stuff legends are made of—"

"Hey!" he interjected. "I'm not—"

"Shut up," she said. "It's been Fargo this and Fargo that ever since I hit St. Louis. Waitresses in Kansas City, smithies in Wichita, drummers on every stage that runs the roads between here and the Mississippi. Face it, Fargo, you're famous. You're a celebrated individual."

One hand crept lower, toward his belt. He was already hard.

"Now, I don't think you got famous because you're tall or good-looking," she went on, "although you certainly are. Or because you ride that fancy horse, or wear these buckskins, or can talk to any savage in his own language. And yes," she added when he lifted a brow, "I heard that, too. But it's not any of those things, is it? It's all that gleaming, spit-shined, solid gold reputation. That's what keeps you up on that pedestal."

He started to argue, but she put two fingers to his lips. "I'm not saying you ever wanted to be up there, or even that you want to be there now. I think it rather embarrasses you. But to a lot of folks, you're high above the crowd. Now it looks like somebody's tried to tarnish that halo of yours, and I'm going to help you polish it back up. And if the trying does me a little good?" She shrugged. "I can live with that. I want to do Daddy and Uncle Tyrone proud."

"And how does making love seal that bargain?" he asked, and immediately wanted to kick himself for a brass-plated idiot.

She smiled up at him, though. "Because it's the only way I know how. Now, take off your pants, darlin'."

Before he had a chance to react, she lifted herself on tiptoes to kiss him, and slid her tongue between his lips.

His arms went around her, pulling her close, and she let out a little moan when her breasts crushed against his chest. Slowly, he slid his hands under her shirttail, up the soft, silky skin of her bare back as he deepened the kiss.

She responded by dropping one hand and insinuating it between their bodies, never taking her lips from his, only working at the buckle of her belt, then his. She freed it, then fumbled at his buttons, and then he was in her soft, warm hand.

His hands dropped then, too, pushing her britches down over her full, round hips. He took her buttocks in both hands, feeling the baby-soft skin sprout into gooseflesh upon exposure to the night-chilled mountain air, then go silky smooth again under the heat of his hands.

Against his mouth, she chuckled, and she broke off the kiss only long enough to whisper, "I feel a draft, Fargo."

Before he could respond, she'd covered his mouth with hers again and was fairly swallowing his tongue. Not that he minded, of course, but a man liked to feel that he had a little more, well, *control* of things.

So he took control.

In one motion, he bent over, shucked her out of her britches, and lifted her off her feet. Her boots went flying off into the grass along with her trousers, but he took little notice of where they went.

"Fargo!" she cried, a little frightened at the suddenness of it, but he lifted her up, kissing her again, and while her mouth was locked to his, he pulled one of her thighs around his waist.

She must have know what was coming, for she brought her other leg up, too, and the instant she locked her legs at his back, he lowered her onto his stiff and waiting shaft.

She was ready for him, slick and hot, and she hissed

in air through her teeth as she sank down upon him.

She seemed weightless in his arms, a confection of night and the dreams that men make in them. He moved her up and down upon himself rhythmically, holding her so close that she was nearly a part of him, then letting her lean back, at arms' length so that their coupling bodies formed a Y, then close again. He felt her nails scratch at his back through the soft buckskin of his shirt, felt her slim grasping hands, and her heated breath at his ear as she whispered, "Yes, Fargo, yes!"

He rocked her, rocked her hard, then slow, then sweet. He felt her tightening around him as her pleas became more urgent. He felt her internal muscles clench around him, squeezing him as she began to spasm, and then he, too, was lost in the void.

And for that moment, she was air, she was so light in his arms: an extension of his climax that seemed to go on and on.

At last, he let her slip from his arms and they slid down into the cool, wet grass together, spent and sated in the darkness. Clementine nestled her head on his chest and sighed.

"By Christ, Fargo," she whispered happily.

He gave her arm a squeeze, then slid his hand underneath her shirt to fondle a breast. She moved her arm to facilitate this, then placed her own hand upon his, through the fabric.

They lay there silently for a time, and then she said, "We're both going to die, you know."

"Don't worry, Clementine. It'll be all right."

She let out a little sigh. "That's what Daddy always said."

"I'm not your Daddy," he whispered, and gave her nipple a soft pinch to underscore the statement.

"No," she said, as she wriggled against him, "you're not."

To his pleasure and surprise, he found he was already hard again. He rolled to his side and unbuttoned Clementine's shirt. She watched him, her eyes still sated, yet playful.

"What are you doing, Fargo?" she asked coyly.

"Those two old goats were so hungry that I didn't get any of that skillet cobbler you slapped together," he said, kissing her nose. In the thin moonlight, her plump, round breasts were shadowed and softly highlighted, their nipples swollen and peaked. He ran his hand around the outside of one, feeling its soft weight, then along the underside. There was nothing so beautiful, to his mind, as the underside of a woman's breast.

He lowered his head and kissed one luscious breast, then the other.

"Fargo?" she whispered. "Why are you babbling about cobbler?"

"I'm going to have my dessert right now," he said, and closed his lips on one pale, puckered nipple.

He suckled her like a baby after mother's milk, first one side, then the other, until she was writhing with want. He didn't give her that thing she craved the most, though, not yet.

First he lapped at her, then tugged at the nipple with his teeth, worrying it like a pup, then sucked it deeply, opening his mouth wide to take in as much of her sweetness as possible.

He licked her chilled flesh, raking his wide tongue over her nipples, then around them, ringing her breasts with feathery kisses before he returned to her erect nipples—hard as sapphires—pulling one into his mouth and nibbling with his teeth, rolling the other between his fingers.

She was wild with want by then, and when he looked up, he saw tears glistening on her cheeks, along the feathery lines of her closed lashes. Not tears of grief, but tears of need, tears of desire.

"Please, Fargo? Please, honey?" She repeated it like a mantra, over and over and over again. Her eyes were clamped shut against her tears, and her breath came in shallow pants.

Only then did he part her legs.

She raised her hips to meet his hand, to meet anything he might offer to fill her need, but he only swept a hand over those soaked, black curls, then rested it on the flat of her belly, rubbing it in slow, small circles.

"You fiend!" she hissed through clenched teeth. "I can't stand it any longer! Please!"

But he returned to her breasts, for they were the

key to her. She'd been wild before, past enthusiastic, but not until he'd begun this love affair with her nipples and with those soft, pillowy breasts had she been so genuinely mindless, so feral. He wondered if she had been accustomed to any foreplay. Maybe Boston shipping magnates didn't believe in it.

Well, he did.

He began to suckle her again, his tongue flicking at her, teasing her, applying pressure, then relieving it. He nipped and bit at the undersides, resting his head on one breast while his mouth played a symphony on the other.

At last, when he was certain she was about to topple, he moved between her legs and hovered at her threshold, letting the head of his manhood come to rest against her entrance. Mindlessly, she pushed herself toward him to try to force his entry, but he moved with her and she didn't succeed.

For a long moment he hovered over her, his weight carried on his arms. She shivered in the grass, whimpering as her wet and glistening nipples puckered in the cool night air with what must be excruciating tightness.

And then, he rammed himself into her quite suddenly, into that luxurious wet velvet that clasped him more firmly than a glove.

She climaxed upon his entry, as he had suspected she would. She spasmed almost maniacally, madly, beneath him, her arms flung wide to the sides and her fingers ripping at the long grass, and he closed his eyes and rode her in earnest, rode the wet, hot wave of her passion until she quieted and rose again.

And they finished together this time, finished so thunderously that he nearly felt the night and the mountains and the tall pines roaring in his ears.

# 10

Zebulon Daggett, owner of the Inca Land and Cattle Company, stood in the morning sunshine at his dining room window, angrily sipping a cup of coffee.

There it was, a scant thirty-eight miles to the south: the legendary Santa Rosa mine. That was, if that idiot Tucker was to be believed.

He scowled.

He looked out over his range, his land. Seventeen thousand acres, owned or leased—or "borrowed." Timberland, grazing land: mountains, streams, and deserts. All his.

Except for that land thirty-eight miles south.

The land he owned stopped roughly ten miles short of the town of Jupiter. The land he leased from the government, at least to the south, barely swallowed up the next three.

Not that his cattle respected any boundaries. The boys had brought steers and cows bearing his brand from as far away as the Rio Salado.

The coffee had grown cold, and he set the cup into its saucer on the tabletop. The hand that placed it there was old and gnarled. He was just beginning to face that, at seventy-three, he wasn't going to live to see the railroad come to take his beef to market, wasn't going to be around when the territory to the south started clamoring for his lumber, wasn't going to live to see his fancy blood horses shipped to buyers all over the country. He had a stud out in his barn that could do the quarter mile faster than he'd ever seen. Never been beat.

But it was neither here nor there. The stud's genes would never pass to more than a few mares, because he'd be dead, too, before they ever saw a railroad.

At the trading post, there was talk of war. This worried him, too. Not that he'd be involved in the conflict. He and his ranch were too far away from Washington, too distant from any land or industries that anybody in their right mind wanted to fight over.

No, he'd just die out here, and then his nephews and nieces could squabble over his holdings. Probably slice up his years of scrimping and saving, of careful management, into seven equal shares, and forget his name five minutes after their portions cleared the bank.

Bunch of spoiled brats, anyway, even if most of them were over forty or fifty by this time. They all had money of their own, anyway. He'd disinherit the lot of them, if only he could think of somebody else to leave it to.

He should have married. He should have had children.

But it was too late now.

"Señor?"

He turned at the sound of his housekeeper's voice. "Yes, Mrs. Vasquez?" She'd been with him for almost twenty years in one capacity or another, but he still addressed her formally.

"I pour more coffee? There is fresh in the kitchen."

He'd forgotten the cup. He eyed it for a moment, then said, "Yes. If you wouldn't mind."

She was about to leave the room when he stopped her. "Mrs. Vasquez, can you tell me why I never married?"

She looked at him for a moment, then shrugged. "Too mean, I guess."

He smiled as she left the room. Leave it to Mrs. Vasquez to tell the truth straight out. Too mean. Yes, he supposed she was right.

Maybe he shouldn't have told Tucker to run those men off. After all, they certainly had more right to whatever silver was there than he did. But old habits died hard. Ordering sheriffs around, displacing people from land he wanted for his cows, acting like the cock of the walk.

"Hell," he whispered to himself. "I *am* the cock of the walk!"

He couldn't help but feel guilty about those miners, though. He'd spoken in haste, hadn't thought it through or been specific enough. He'd awakened last night in a sweat, hoping that Tucker and his deputies hadn't actually hurt them.

Hurt them! This, from a man who had routinely strung up rustlers, and who had, two times in his life, killed without regret men stupid enough to try to homestead on his land.

"You *are* getting old," he muttered. "You're getting worried about God."

He looked out, past the wide clearing with its corrals and barns and outbuildings, to the tall ponderosa pines; looked through them to the thin blue sky.

But the miners were gone by now, and he supposed it wouldn't hurt anything to let people keep on thinking that mine was on his land—hell, the gossip had him up to fifty thousand acres, give or take.

"Señor Daggett?"

He jumped a little, and his chest fluttered ominously. Mrs. Vasquez was at his shoulder with the coffee. Lately she'd been able to sneak up on him more than he liked.

But his heart settled almost immediately, and he took the cup without comment. He said, "Send word to Mr. Shepherd, please. I want to see him."

Luke Shepherd was his foreman. He'd ride down

there with Shepherd, and maybe take six or eight men, too. No wagons, yet. First, he wanted to have a look-see at this mine he didn't own, make sure that Tucker hadn't taken leave of his senses.

The lost Santa Rosa Mine indeed!

Well, stranger things had happened. If it was true, he could leave the extra men to guard it, and maybe they could break a few more rocks while they waited for him to figure out how to best get the ore out and freighted to the closest smelter. New Mexico, perhaps? It would be quite a long haul.

He carried his coffee out of the dining room, through the foyer, and to his white-washed and fancy-spindled front porch to wait for Mr. Shepherd. What would happen to this house when he died, this grand, rambling house he had built piece by piece, with shipments of glass and brass and bric-a-brac coming for two years from back East, and his men planing boards for walls, for flooring, for rafters, and the masons laying brick and stone?

He should have had children. A son or a daughter able to appreciate the fine things he'd brought to this clearing in the forest, and the brains to shepherd his outfit once he was gone.

He should have had children.

Fargo's group headed slowly south.

They'd left the last of the pine forest behind them a good hour ago, and now only an isolated thrust of rock or the occasional scrub cypress or juniper graced the rolling lowlands.

Clementine had been in a good mood when they started out, humming as she tacked up her mule and they started down through the trees. But as the long morning had worn on, Fargo had noticed a distinct absence of singing.

"You okay?" he'd asked her, about an hour ago.

"Fine," she'd said with a terse nod. "Just fine." And then she'd given him a smile.

*Liar,* he thought. He figured that the reality of what they were about to do had hit home.

"Sure you don't want to go back and catch the stage?" he'd asked.

Her smile had changed into a grimace of determination, and she'd kicked her mule to catch up to the others.

When they'd stopped for a bite and to rest the horses around midday, she'd pulled him over behind a copse of cedar trees and given him a long kiss that had nearly melted the buckskins right off of him.

He'd caught a handful of breast—actually, he'd caught a quick mouthful—before Weasel came looking for them.

Clementine had quickly pulled her shirt down and handed out the jerky, calm as you please.

But they hadn't talked—outside of "pass the water"—since.

Weasel Smith had enough stories to keep the air filled with words, though. He talked about the old days, when there was nobody out here but him and ten thousand Indians, to hear him tell it. He talked about the old days of trapping, when the beaver were still plentiful and a man could make himself a fortune in furs.

He spoke of Rendezvous, about how all the trappers from near and far would meet up in one location to get a taste of civilization—or at least, human company—and how he met his first wife there, a Cheyenne woman named Lonely Willow.

"You sort'a put me in mind of her, ma'am," he said to Clementine. "All that long dark hair, and the way she rode a horse. Proud-like. 'Course," he added, "she didn't have no blue eyes."

"What happened to her?" Clementine asked.

"The small pox took her," he replied thoughtfully.

"She died not two years after we was wed. Well, sort'a wed, dependin' on how you fancy your ceremonies. Anyhow, our baby girl died with her. Mary Ann. She were just a year old."

Clementine reined in. "Oh, Mr. Smith! I'm so sorry!"

He shrugged. "It were a long time ago. Had me three wives since then, more or less official. Mostly less official, I guess," he added with a grin. "No more young'uns, though. Now Lush here is a different story entire, ain't you, Lush?"

Lush grunted.

"Lush used to be a bookkeeper, if'n you can believe that," Weasel crowed. "An ink-spotted, figure-tottin' bookkeeper in Virginy!"

Lush colored and Weasel went on with another story while Fargo mulled over his plans for the next few days. Right now, that was as far ahead as he was prepared to think.

It had occurred to him, about twenty minutes into Weasel's dissertation on the foibles of adding up columns of figures in stuffy rooms—and why Lush was better off trapping and getting his leg smashed up in the fresh air—that he had better worm his way into their conversation. They were only about a half an hour from the mine as it was, and he was dead sure that the last thing they should do was ride right in there like they owned the place.

"Weasel?" he said.

Nobody paid him any mind.

"Weasel!" he shouted.

Weasel turned toward him. "You say somethin' Fargo?"

"Yeah. I think we'd better be talking about where we're going."

Weasel rolled his eyes. "Well, we're going down to Jupiter, in case you hadn't noticed."

"No, we're not," Fargo said. "You boys had better know that I'm wanted in town."

"Tucker lookin' for you, is he?" Weasel cackled.

Fargo nodded. "For killing Clementine's father and uncle."

Clementine threw him a look, and hurriedly interjected, "He didn't do it, Mr. Smith. I can assure you of that. The sheriff and his deputy—or deputies—did. I was there. I heard them."

"Now don't get me wrong, ma'am," Weasel said. "I ain't got no time for Farley Tucker. But why in tarnation would he up and kill your papa and uncle, little lady?" Doubt edged his voice.

"Because Daddy and Uncle Tyrone were those miners," she said. "The ones you heard Mr. Daggett tell Sheriff Tucker to get rid of."

A silence fell over the group for the first time since daybreak, and the only sounds were those of leather creaking, and of hooves trudging over the gravely dust and swishing brittle weeds.

Finally, Lush Fillpot spoke. "I believe I'd like to see this mine," he said softly.

"Well," announced Weasel with a sudden grin, "whatever Lush says, goes. I reckon we're off to see your mine. Or Old Man Daggett's mine. Kinda like to take a piece outta Farley Tucker's hide, my own dang self!"

# 11

Over Weasel Smith's repeated offers to "take a piece outta Farley Tucker's hide," Fargo talked the old trapper into staying behind with the others while he rode the Ovaro ahead. He stopped at the base of the rise that overlooked the spring and the mine, from where he'd spied on the deputy before—the same deputy that he now was convinced was Clay Reeves.

Spyglass in hand, he ground-tied the stallion and crawled to the top of the rise on his belly, brushing away a scorpion as he went.

He'd half-expected there'd be no one there. After all, Reeves had ridden out only yesterday to nose around—doubtless, looking for him. Fargo had figured he'd cool his heels back in town for at least a week. Besides, it would raise suspicion if a third of the town's law enforcers disappeared for the whole day, every day.

But it seemed greed was stronger than common sense. Not only was Reeves down there, but the sheriff was with him, and they were both carrying shiny new picks and shovels into the mine.

Well, this sure as hell threw two hitches into the plowline, Fargo decided.

Fargo wormed his way down the slope, mounted the Ovaro, and set out at walk for the place where he'd left the others.

"You're going to have to wait here for a spell," he

said, dismounting beside one of the yuccas that formed a small grove. Several similar groves dotted the gently rolling desert landscape. "You might as well get comfortable."

Clementine rose from the cast shadow of her mule and fanned dust from her britches. "Why? What's wrong?"

"Just about everything," he said. He pulled down his canteen and unscrewed the cap. "They're mining it, the idiots."

"Who's minin' it?" piped up Weasel.

"The sheriff and Reeves," Fargo said after he took a drink. "At least, I think it's Reeves. They're lugging picks and shovels and stone chisels and God-knows-what else down the shaft right now."

Weasel's old eyes sparkled mischievously. "Jus' the two of 'em?"

"Oh, no you don't," warned Clementine. She turned toward Fargo and said adamantly, "I'm not about to avenge Daddy's death that way. Uncle Tyrone's either. I don't want blood on my hands."

Fargo suddenly developed a whole new respect for her.

"Well, what do you folks suggest?" Weasel asked, incredulously. "You wanna jus' forget the whole dang thing? Hell's bells, I were countin' on gettin' to see the inside'a that mine. Not often a feller comes across a fable made truth!" He turned toward Fargo and stuck his thumb back toward Clementine. "She was tellin' us how her daddy and uncle found all them old powdery bones down there, and about the rings what was drove into the stone. I got a mind to see that!"

Fargo held up a hand. The old coot was dead serious and half-riled, and he figured it would be easier to settle him down with good humor than a fist. Weasel might be pushing sixty, but he looked like he could wrestle a grizzly and end up with a bearskin coat.

"Whoa there, friend!" he said with a smile. "You'll

get your chance for a peek. It's just going to be a spell, that's all. If I'm right, they'll leave well before dark, because it's a long ride back to town."

"And what makes you figger they'll go back?" Weasel asked testily.

"They'll have to show up there," Fargo said, "because right at the moment Tucker's got one lame deputy watching the whole shebang. Not that there's a whole lot of lawbreaking in Jupiter—and not that there are many people to break it—but he's got to keep up appearances."

Weasel stood down. "You think that other deputy is in on it, too?"

"I honestly don't know," Fargo said, although he had his doubts about Josh Simpson. The deputy who had come to his room in town didn't seem the murderous type. Stupid, but not murderous.

"Weasel?" said Lush.

"What we've got to do now," Fargo said, "is—"

"Weasel?" Lush again.

"Dang it anyway! What is it, Lush?" Weasel said. "He's always flappin' his lips, Fargo. About talks me to death sometimes."

Lush pointed out across the desert to several distant shapes, moving obliquely across the plain. "We've got company."

"Get back behind the yuccas," Fargo snapped. "Now! The horses and mules, too." He pulled his spyglass from his saddlebag and sighted down on the riders.

"Who is it?" Clementine hissed. "Is it that snake Daggett?"

"No," replied Fargo grimly. He moved the glass from the end of the column to the front. Five riders, leading two steers, plodded along the horizon. He let the spyglass drop from his eye and dangle in his hand.

"Well, who is it, then?" demanded Clementine, tugging at his sleeve.

Fargo just kept staring toward the horizon, his mouth set into a hard line. "Apaches."

They waited.

The line of riders continued to move slowly, paying them no mind if, indeed, they'd spotted them there behind the yuccas. Fargo figured they hadn't. If the Apaches had seen them, they'd be minus their livestock by now at the very least. He spoke Apache, but he didn't count on a man of them to give him time to get out a word or greeting. Not when there was livestock to steal.

The line disappeared from time to time behind a rise, only to appear at the other end of it, still moving at the same plodding pace.

"Why don't they speed up?" Clementine said. She was huddled in the thin purple shade of two yuccas, arms wrapped around her knees, as she had been for the last thirty minutes.

"Reckon they don't want to wear out them cattle, ma'am," Weasel offered. He was stretched out on the ground, his floppy hat pulled low over his eyes.

"I've knowed them Apache to make seventy miles in a day, when they was of a mind to," Weasel continued. "'Course, I ain't allowin' the first horse made but thirty of it."

Fargo had the spyglass up again. "They're turning."

"Toward us?" Clementine said, a note of barely controlled hysteria creeping into her voice.

He dropped a hand to her shoulder and gave it a squeeze. "Toward the mine," he said. "Probably going to the spring."

"That'd be for the livestock," Weasel said, his face still hidden by his hat. "Why, I've heard tell about how they make them young Apache boys run for miles an' miles with a whole mouthful of water, just holdin' it, and make 'em spit it out when they get done. It's a test, like."

Weasel's running commentary wasn't doing much for Clementine, who blanched. She said, "Those men are at the mine."

Fargo nodded. He also knew that they'd left their mounts hobbled beside the spring, in full view.

"Well, it's just too dang bad for 'em," Weasel went on. "Likely, they'll let 'em off with just their eyelids slit, or maybe their privates cut off. Pardon me for sayin' it, ma'am."

Clementine's eyes went wide in shock, but Weasel just kept on talking. "You'd be surprised what a feller can live through, though. Why, once, I came across a white feller tied up to a tree with his privates hacked off and stuck in his mouth, and danged if he weren't still alive."

Fargo said, "Weasel."

"Well, I got the bleedin' stopped and found me some sound reeds, all little and hollow like, to stick up there for him to piss through," Weasel continued, as if he hadn't heard. "To hold the path open, you might say. Shock of it nigh on to killed him. Well, that and the blood loss. But the son of a bitch lived. Last I heard, he was—"

"Weasel!"

"—trappin' up on the Salmon River under the name of Peckerless Peterson." He lifted his hat and looked up at Fargo. "What?"

"Just shut up," Fargo said. "You're scaring the lady."

Weasel flicked an eye toward Clementine, whose position had gone from hunched over to nearly fetal. He said, "Oh. Sorry, ma'am. No offense."

From the shade of the horses, Lush muttered, "Jesus, Weasel."

Clementine moaned softly.

Fargo went over to her and crouched beside her and hugged her rounded shoulders. "Nothing we can do, darlin','' he said. He stroked her hair. It was like silk beneath his fingers.

She lifted a teary face to his, and whispered, "Those Indians will torture them, Fargo. I'm as much for justice as the next person, but torturing someone and cutting off their . . . their . . ."

"They might not, ma'am," Weasel ventured. "Sometimes they just skin a feller alive. 'Course, that takes a few days if you does it right. Now, I heard about a fella down around the border country that them savages they strung from a tree upside down, and lit a fire under his head—"

At the same time, both Fargo and Lush hissed, "Weasel!"

Sniffing, Clementine looked over at the old trapper, then back at Fargo. "Having your skin peeled off is a long way from twenty years to life at Yuma." She began to cry in earnest.

He didn't have any comfort to offer her, so he did the only thing he could. He gave her shoulders a last little squeeze, then stood up and went to the Ovaro. The Indians had disappeared behind the roll of the land. They wouldn't see him. He mounted up.

"Fargo, what the hell are you doing?" Clementine said, suddenly unfolding herself and leaping to her feet. She was at his side in an instant, and clinging to his leg. "Don't go, please! Don't go anywhere near them!"

Ignoring Clementine, he asked Weasel, "You boys got plenty of ammunition?"

"I'm ready for 'er," Weasel said, and slapped the pistol strapped to his thigh. Lush gave a quick nod of his head.

"Let go, Clem," Fargo said.

"No!" she wept. "Not until you promise me—"

He reached down and pried her hands away. "I'm just going to go take a look, that's all. I'll be fine."

Roughly, she scrubbed at her eyes with a hand.

"Then why'd you ask about them having enough ammunition?"

All four heads turned toward the south at the distant report of a firearm.

"Oh, God," breathed Clementine.

Another shot rang out.

"I'll be fine," Fargo said, and rode out before she had a chance to grab his leg again.

# 12

This time, Fargo left the Ovaro farther out and crept cautiously to the rise where he'd kept watch before. He brought along the Henry as well as the spyglass this time, and as he silently slithered the last few feet up to the crest, he kept the Henry at the ready.

There were seven horses at the spring, along with two cattle and a mule. He supposed another one of McBrides' string had wandered back. There had been no other shots fired since those first two, and there were no signs of human life.

No signs, that is, unless a man knew where—and how—to look.

He spied the first brave down in the shadow of a patch of palo verde, but it took him a second to see the second man, crouched beside him. Number three was out of sight—that was, all but one mocassin and a bit of leather legging, which peeped from behind a pile of boulders. Fargo wouldn't have spotted it if the man hadn't moved to adjust his position.

He could see nothing of number four other than just the edge of a pale orange head sash. It caught the light at the mouth of the tunnel. He was inside it, waiting—for number five, Fargo supposed—who was probably down in the shafts, scouting.

The four men outside had their backs turned toward him, and Fargo was careful not to give them a reason to turn around. He was fairly sure that even if they did, he was high enough up—and close enough to the ground—that he'd be invisible to them.

Still, he'd learned long ago that you couldn't be too careful with Apaches.

This was a party that had gone out after food, and they'd landed what looked liked a couple of Daggett's steers. He couldn't make out the brand from this distance, but who else ranched cattle around this part of the territory?

So it wasn't a war party. They weren't painted or dressed for it. No, this meeting with Tucker and Reeves was just a happy accident, at least from the braves' point of view. They thought they'd pick up a couple of extra horses and a mule, and whatever weapons and food the lawmen had on them.

Right now, Fargo figured he was mightily happy that he wasn't in Tucker's boots.

Of course, you never could tell about the Apache. They might haul those boys out of the mine and spend a couple days skinning them, just for the sheer pleasure of it. Then again, they might check out the shaft and decide it wasn't worth chancing a few thousand tons of rock coming down on their heads just for a little fun. In that case, they'd most likely steal the livestock and head on home.

Unless there were a couple of hotheaded young bucks among them.

Just then, the one standing at the mouth of the shaft jumped. It startled Fargo, and he jumped a little, too, but not nearly so much as he did a split second later when a shot rang out, soft and muffled by the hillside.

Immediately, the fifth brave tumbled out of the shaft, into the sunshine, followed by a billowing cloud of roiling dust.

As the shaft continued to vomit dust, the four other braves came out of hiding and regrouped at the spring, chattering wildly. If Fargo had been closer, he would have understood what was said. As it was, he could only watch them gesturing through his spyglass.

That, and worry about what had gone on inside the mine shaft.

Five minutes later, the Apaches must have decided it wasn't worth their while, for they gathered up the horses and the steers and the mule and set off south at a brisk trot.

As he watched them disappear over the horizon, he was faced with a fresh dilemma: go down and try to dig those boys out—for that dust could have been nothing else but a cave-in—or go back to get Clementine and the old trappers.

He wasn't wild about the idea of digging. Sheriff Tucker hadn't done much to make him seem worthy of saving, and Deputy Reeves had gone out of his way to prove his hide wasn't worth a plug nickel. And then there'd be the problem of what to do with them, even if he did get them out alive.

Besides, Fargo didn't know to what extent the mine had caved in.

He stewed on this for a minute, tugging at his beard, and then said, "Aw, hell."

He grabbed his Henry and slithered down the slope, feet first.

Three men could dig faster than one. He'd go back for the others.

It was sweaty work.

They labored into the night, with bandannas tied over their mouths and noses to keep them from choking on so much dust. Muscles straining, they passed rocks like firefighters might pass buckets between the trough and the conflagration.

Reeves and Tucker had been in the cave Clementine called the "ore room" when they had fired the slug that did the damage, for it was that end of the shaft system that was caved in. Fargo figured they'd have to tunnel maybe twenty-five or thirty feet more—on top of the ten they'd already cleared—before they reached them.

And they heard no signs of life. Not a peep.

"I'll bet your J. Robert Sykes never showed you a time like this," Fargo said to Clementine when it was his turn to take a breather outside beside the little fire they'd built.

She said nothing, just wiped the dust from his brow, then handed him a cup of coffee and a plate of cold beans and bread. There hadn't been time for her to cook, as she was moving rocks, too.

She made no comment, just sat there against him, watching him eat. He was almost finished when she asked, "Do you think they're still alive? How much air does a man need to breathe, anyway?"

He took a long drink of coffee. "If the cave itself didn't come down, they've got plenty of air to take them well into tomorrow. That is, if they didn't get caught in the shaft. They could be dead right now. We could be tunneling back to corpses."

She looked away. "I wish you'd stop candy-coating everything, Fargo," she said.

He smiled, although he didn't know why. He needed at least one of them alive to clear his name. He had Clementine's word, of course, but the word of a women—and a stranger to the town, at that—wasn't going to count for much when it came right down to it.

"Don't worry, Clem," he said, as much to balm his own fears as to quell hers. "We'll get to 'em by daylight if we keep up this pace. 'Course, they're going to have to walk back to town."

He thought he heard a small chuckle escape her. "Serves 'em right," she whispered.

Just then, the ground began to rumble.

He jumped to his feet, bringing Clementine with

him, and they both leapt back just as a new billow of dust belched from the tunnel's mouth.

Weasel and Lush stumbled out in the middle of it, coughing and hacking, and accompanied by the roar of a fresh cave-in.

Weasel sputtered, "Crikey!" between choked coughs.

"What happened?" Fargo asked, helping the men to their feet.

As if he didn't know. Every time he thought he might have a handle on this thing, it took a new turn for the worse.

"Well," said Weasel, clearing his throat for the third or fourth time, "you remember that fifteen feet or so that we cleared?"

Fargo nodded.

"She's down again, and maybe five or ten feet more. Solid."

Clementine shoved a cup of water into Weasel's hands, and he took a long slug. She gave a cup to Lush, too, but he seemed too shaken to drink.

"We're going to need help," he said.

Weasel nodded.

"But there isn't anybody!" Clementine said. "There's nobody for miles and miles, and you can't go into Jupiter, Fargo!"

"No, but you can."

She blinked. "Me?"

"You and Lush," he said. Lush could get her there quicker, and provide some protection once they were in town. He'd said he had kin in Jupiter, and maybe they'd help. Besides, the deputy would listen with a keener ear to a man than a woman.

"Lush can go by himself," she announced, crossing her arms.

"Lush'll be busy putting together a rescue party," he said. "I've got other business for you to take care of."

"But, Fargo—"

"You're going," he insisted, "and you're going to take my horse."

" 'Scuse me?" spoke up Weasel.

"Don't you order me around!" shouted Clementine. "I can move rocks almost as good as you can. Well, nearly. It seems to me that you'll need every extra hand you can get, and furthermore—"

"Ain't nobody going nowhere for a couple'a hours, folks," Weasel broke in.

He was right. The slivered moon, which earlier had hung high in the sky, was fully cloaked by clouds. The surrounding desert was cloaked in unrelenting black. Fargo knew it would be foolhardy to send out riders into the pitch.

"All right," he said. "Dawn." He dug into a pocket and found his watch, and bent to hold it to the flickering firelight. It was a good bit later than he had thought. "It's a quarter past three," he said, slipping it back into his pocket. "We're all beat out, and those two in the shaft aren't going anywhere. I suggest we all get a few hours' sleep."

"Fine by me," said Weasel, who was already crawling toward his blankets.

Fargo scooped up his bedding, and Clementine's, and then took her wrist and dragged her out of the camp, down by the spring.

She fought him on it, although the fight was more for show than for real, he suspected.

"Damn you, Fargo!" she spat once he'd dropped their blankets and let go of her. "I'm not riding into Jupiter! I want to stay here and help!"

"Now, Clem . . ." he soothed. He dropped to his knees and began spreading out the blankets into one big, soft bed.

She didn't notice. "I will not be sent away like some idiot child!" she railed. "You won't send me off to Boston—I mean, Jupiter—I mean . . . Oh, fiddle." She slumped to the ground. "Well," she said lamely, "I won't go."

Fargo patted the last blanket into place, then sat down in the middle of the makeshift pallet. He held out his hand. "Come here, Clem."

She joined him, although somewhat reluctantly, he thought.

"I'm not just sending you off to get rid of you," he said when she sat down.

She eyed him, one brow arched. "You're not?"

"There's something I want you to do in town, and only you can do it."

"And that is?"

He pulled her close. "Why don't you shuck out of those clothes," he whispered, "and I'll tell you."

# 13

Past thousands of tons of rock, Clay Reeves sat in darkness, waiting for the end.

A while ago he'd thought he'd heard a sound, just a faint one, and he'd brightened. He'd even started making up stories to explain how Tucker had died. It had to have been somebody from town out there, trying to dig them out. Apaches wouldn't bother.

But the sound turned out to be nothing but the precursor to a second cave-in. That one had been farther away, only shaking down more ancient dust into his nostrils as he waited to die, his back pressed up against the piles of ore left by ancient, murdered Spaniards.

Tucker lay somewhere beyond his outstretched feet. He'd been hit by falling rocks. Probably would have made it, too, if they'd had any hope of rescue. But they didn't, and Reeves had strangled the rest of the life out of him.

Tucker had put up a hell of good fight for a man with a broken arm, which Clay Reeves's aching temple could attest to. How could he know the son of a bitch had a rock in his hand?

But he'd found his grip and choked Tucker until the bastard stopped moving. Just taking up air, that's all he was doing, air that rightfully belonged to Reeves.

God damn those thieving Apaches, anyway! He supposed his horse was probably their dinner by now. He hoped they choked to death.

But then lately, all his thoughts had turned to death.

He would have stabbed himself, but all he had was a pocketknife, and one with a short blade at that, worn to impossible thinness by too many idle whettings over too many years.

He would have shot himself, except that he was certain it'd bring down the roof of the small cave. And what if he didn't kill himself right off? Suppose the slug glanced off his skull?

He didn't want to be crushed to death, to lie there in agony before death came in its own sweet time to claim him. Anything but that.

He kicked one leg into the void, and his boot connected with Tucker's shin. He supposed it was his shin, anyway. The stupid peckerwood. Five years back, he'd seen Tucker shoot a man in cold blood. Not much of a man, but a man nonetheless. He hadn't really thought much about it at the time, but then he rode into Jupiter three years later and recognized Tucker, the sheriff, as the same man who'd done the shooting.

Well, a man could use a steady paycheck for a change. It beat bushwhacking pilgrims for pocket change.

If the places had been reversed, if he'd been Tucker, he would have just shot the man and got on with sheriffing. But fortunately for him—and unfortunately for Tucker—the sheriff had a guilty streak. It was thin, but it was there.

"Give me a job or I'll spill the beans," he'd said, or words to that effect, and so, for the past two years, he'd been Jupiter's number one deputy.

You had to play a fine line with blackmail.

He blinked, and the inside of his eyelids were almost brighter than the outside. He wished there was water. He wished he could see something. It was a rotten end, especially considering what it might have been.

He waited.


"Señor? Señor Daggett?"

It took him a second to realize that it was Mrs. Vasquez calling to him.

He opened one eye. It was still dark.

"What?" he said, grumpily.

"You leave in an hour, señor."

That was right. He was riding south this morning, going to go see about that mine. He sat up, his old bones recounting every insult from the last sixty or seventy years, then silently, grudgingly, letting them go.

It was hell getting old. But then, he'd thought that at forty, too. Christ! Forty was young—practically a kid! At least, it was from the perspective he now held.

Mrs. Vasquez silently turned and padded toward the kitchen, taking her lamplight with her. He threw the covers back, feeling the sudden chill, but giving it no power over him, he sat up. He groped for a few moments on his nightstand, then found the sulphur tips. He struck one and lit his lamp.

The hearth was cold. His fire had gone out in the night—an oversight on his part—and he made a mental note to put in more firewood.

He shoved his feet into cold slippers, stood, made his way to the chifforobe, and began to dress.

He was just buttoning up his shirt when the sickness started to come on him again. Swearing and gripping his arm, which had begun to ache and throb, he staggered toward the bed and sat down in a heap.

Sweat beading his brow as he waited, teeth clenched, for the pounding in his chest to quiet, for the shooting pains to stop. And finally, the agony eased.

He sat there, panting. Each time, it was a little longer, a little more severe.

He mopped his brow. His shirt was soaked through with sweat, and he pulled it off. The chill on his skin felt good for a change. At least it didn't hurt. It reminded him he was still alive.

He sat there panting for a good five minutes, and then he stood up again and found a fresh shirt.

He hadn't told anybody about these little seizures, as he called them. There'd been four of them just this year, and they were getting closer together, now. But he didn't want anybody to think he was weak, or that his health was failing. He hadn't even told that quack Doc Martin, up at the trading post.

"Probably just tell me to quit drinking," he grumbled as he buttoned up the shirt. "That's his answer to everything. Well, *he* oughta stop drinking, that's the way I see it. Don't know how a man can pretend to practice medicine when he's always three sheets to the wind . . ."

By the time he was dressed and ready to face breakfast, he was feeling fairly chipper, although not particularly hungry. Best eat something, though. He had a long ride ahead of him.

# 14

In the thin, breaking light of dawn, Fargo saw Lush Fillpot and Clementine off to town. He'd put Clementine on the Ovaro. He watched her now, just a speck on the black-and-white stallion, cantering out of sight into the early-morning gloom.

"Fargo?" Weasel crouched behind him. "You gonna stand there all day staring at that gal's backside, or are we gonna get to movin' rocks?"

Fargo turned and joined Weasel at the mouth of the shaft. Carrying lanterns, they started down.

"Reckon you can wait here," Weasel said when they were halfway to the edge of the rockfall. "I'll haul 'em out this far, then you can haul 'em the rest of the way."

Fargo didn't argue with him. Either job was just as backbreaking. Yesterday, they'd amassed quite a heap of rock, piled at the edge of camp. There looked to be quite a good bit of high-grade ore in it, as a matter of fact, but nobody had remarked on it. They were all too busy trying to get to the men trapped behind it.

"How much more air them fellers got left, you reckon?" Weasel asked.

Fargo set down his lantern and shook his head. "Maybe late afternoon. Maybe till evening. But not much more."

"Bunch'a murderin' claim jumpers," Weasel grumbled as he walked away, lantern swinging. "That's what they are. If'n it was me, I'd just let 'em die back there. That's their just deserts. Ain't right, a man havin' to move rock and rock and more rock two days in a row on their cowardly, backshootin' account. And on only three hours' sleep." In no time, Weasel came trudging up the shaft with the first rock, and handed it off to him. He almost went to the ground with it, and struggled back up with his feet braced and his shoulders straining.

From there on out, there was nothing but the work, and his aching back, and the sweat dripping from his brow. That, and the occasional thought of Clementine's journey east, to Jupiter.

Lush wasn't much company.

The gray-bearded trapper hadn't said more than three words to her, and by her reckoning they were almost halfway to Jupiter. It was all right, though. It gave her time to think.

She slowed the Ovaro down to a fast walk, the fourth time she'd done so since they started. He was truly a magnificent beast and still seemed fresh, but she wanted to take no chances with him. She didn't like to think what Fargo might say if she rode his horse into the ground. Besides, Lush's mount seemed to be laboring.

She slowed the Ovaro down to a plod. The stallion shook his head, rattling his bridle softly, as if to say he still had plenty of run in him. She patted his neck, but held him back. There was no sense in ruining Lush's horse, either.

The sun was well up over the horizon, and riding into its harsh light hurt her eyes. She wished she'd borrowed Fargo's hat, too.

Fargo. The man was like an opiate to her. She couldn't get enough of him, couldn't stop thinking about him.

She wished she'd never crossed paths with him.

It wasn't fair, that was all there was to it. She'd come West thinking to put the past behind her, to start over again, fresh, and to help her father. She'd seen herself in a simple dress, flipping flapjacks or frying chicken in the kitchen of a rustic little picket-fenced house in an idealized western town. Of which, she'd realized five minutes after seeing the real West, there were exactly none.

No houses with white picket fences, no rose gardens or twining ivy, no kindly neighbors stopping to pass the time. At least, not here.

And just when she'd found a man—*the* man—who could make her happy, who didn't care about her past, who played her body like a finely tuned instrument, she realized that he wouldn't stay around. Men like Fargo never did. He loved her in his way, but that's all it was—his way. He'd leave.

She bore him no malice for this. She could no more make him stay than she could nail the wind to a tree, no more than she could stop the sun from rising or the rain from falling.

So she began to think over her possibilities.

She had some money in the bank. Not much, but enough for a start. But at what? Dressmaking? She couldn't mend so much as a sock without soaking it in her own blood.

Teaching school? They investigated schoolteachers, and her past wouldn't bear up under any scrutiny at all.

Waiting tables? She sniffed derisively. Under no circumstances would she work on her feet all day for tips in some greasy hash house, getting her backside spanked by every fellow who thought that the price of a meal entitled him to maul the serving girl.

There was always whoring, but she'd only ever had two lovers in her life: J. Robert Sykes, and now Fargo. She couldn't bend that into a life of dirty trappers and crooked gamblers and grimy miners, no matter how she tried. The idea of consorting for pay with the flotsam and jetsam of life sickened her.

Maybe she could go to a big town, like San Francisco. Maybe there would be an opportunity there for a young woman with no family, but more than a few smarts. And a finishing school education. Don't forget that.

The horses seemed rested, and she glanced over at Lush. She found him staring not at the trail ahead, but square at her bustline.

She sighed. Young or old, citified or rustic, all men were basically the same, weren't they?

"Mr. Fillpot?" she said, and his head came up. He blinked. "Mr. Fillpot, are you ready for a little speed?"

He nodded, and he had the decency to look a tad guilty. He kicked his mount into a gallop and headed out.

Momentarily holding back the Ovaro, she gave her head a little shake. Lush Fillpot was a cast-iron, died-in-the-wool eccentric, all right—Weasel Smith, too—but they were surely dear old things.

"All right, fella," she said to Fargo's horse, who was jittering beneath her, eager to catch up to the bay cantering out ahead. "Let's ride," she said, and showed the Ovaro her heels.

In the hard, relentless darkness of the little cave, Clay Reeves rose from a fitful doze. It had grown stuffy over the last few hours. It wasn't hard to breathe yet, but he supposed it would only be a matter of time.

He shot out a leg again, checking to see if Tucker's body was still there. It was, and he was relieved. Twice now he'd dreamt that he hadn't really killed the sheriff, and that Tucker was creeping around behind him, a pickax poised overhead and ready to strike.

That was just plain silly, Reeves told himself. They'd

lost the pickax somewhere back there, somewhere underneath all those rocks.

Still, he couldn't help but shiver.

His bones were cold from more than the thought of Tucker's return from the dead, though. He was sitting on rock, rock that was deep underground and cold as ice. Last night—was it during the night? He didn't know, had no way to, and he didn't want to use his last sulphur tip to check his watch—he'd had to get up and walk in circles in the darkness, just to keep his circulation going.

Now, that was a laugh! Why should he worry about his circulation when he was going to be dead as a post in a few hours?

He'd tripped over Tucker a few times, tripped again over the ore, and cursing it, sat himself down again. He hadn't moved since.

At least the cold would keep Tucker from smelling to high heaven when he started to rot. That was the last thing he needed, to be trapped down in the same hole with a stinking corpse.

But then, he'd be dead by then, wouldn't he?

In the darkness, he began to sing, although he was scarcely aware of it. The old seafaring chant that crossed his lips, taught to him long ago by his maternal grandfather, who had sailed around the world in whaling ships, seemed to be sung as much in his own head as through his lips.

" 'Farewell and adieu to you fair Spanish ladies,' " he sang softly, the sound of his dry and scratchy baritone voice echoing, just slightly, and magnified by the unforgiving and solid rock walls of his stone prison. " 'Farewell and adieu to you ladies of Spain. . . .' "

# 15

At just past nine o'clock, Clementine and Lush rode into Jupiter and jogged down the dusty main road, looking for the sheriff's office.

It was a tiny town, Clementine thought. In fact, it was hardly a town at all. It was much smaller than her father had led her to believe, although a big town to him and a big town to her must, of course, have been two separate things. But there couldn't be more than two hundred souls in the whole place, if that!

Despite its small population, the town of Jupiter seemed to support a number of businesses. They rode past three slapped-together saloons—the only scenes of any activity at all—a goodly number of weedy and dusty vacant lots, a combination mercantile and dry goods, what looked like a bank and barbershop under one roof, and a livery stable before they found what they were looking for.

Clementine tied the Ovaro to the hitching rail and followed Lush up the step, to the open door. *After we tell the deputy,* she thought, *I'll ask around. They'd know at the bank, wouldn't they?*

They stepped inside, but there was no deputy. The jail was as deserted as the street had been.

"Perfect," she said to Lush. "Why isn't the law ever around when you need—"

"Where'd you folks get this horse?" came a voice

from the doorway. "This spotted horse tied at the rail."

She turned around, and was relieved to see a tall man in the doorway, a badge glinting on his chest.

"I borrowed him," she began. Now that she'd found the deputy, she realized she had so much to tell him that she didn't know where to start. "Our friend, Skye Fargo, is out at—"

"Your friend?" the deputy said with a scowl, and drew his pistol.

Involuntarily, Clementine took a step back, and bumped into Lush.

"Put all your weapons on the desk, real careful," the deputy said. "Then back away slow, over to the wall. Hands where I can see 'em."

Clementine, being unarmed, backed to the wall immediately. It took Lush a bit longer to divest himself. His rifle and handgun came first, followed by two skinning knives, a long thin blade down his boot, and a derringer, which was secreted in his racoon hat. And all the while, he seemed to be studying the deputy's face.

"Why, Mr. Fillpot!" Clementine exclaimed in surprise at about the time he found the second knife. "You were carrying an arsenal the whole time, and you never said a thing!"

"Yes, ma'am," he muttered, head down. He backed to the wall to join her. "Better safe than bushwacked and scalped, is what I say."

"Hush your mouth, old-timer," the deputy barked. "Keep your hands out to your sides where I can see 'em, both of you. Now, where's the murderin' trash who owns that horse?"

Clementine rolled her eyes. "I should hardly call him 'murdering trash'! And I would have told you. You don't need to keep pointing that gun at us."

"Tell me now," he demanded, and wiggled the nose of his revolver at them.

She stomped a foot. "Be quiet and give me a chance, all right? He's at the mine, trying to dig that murdering sheriff and deputy out from under a cave-in, that's where he is! We came to put together a rescue party, and while you're busy playing around with your gun they're probably suffocating, which is fine and good with me because they killed my daddy and Uncle Tyrone, the low-down swine!"

By the time she finished, she was shouting and her face was hot, and Lush had taken her hand and was patting it.

The deputy's reply to her outburst, however, was to wiggle his gun again. "In the cell," he said.

Clementine snatched her hand back from Lush. "I will not!" she snapped. "Didn't you hear a word I said?"

The deputy looked a little confused, but held his ground. "I heard you, miss. But that ain't the same as believin' you. Now, go on, the both of you. Move, old-timer." He took a step toward them.

But Lush, much to Clementine's surprise, stepped not toward the cell, but toward the deputy. "Don't be shaming me, boy," he growled.

The deputy stopped in his tracks. "Quit talkin' crazy. And don't come no closer."

"I know I haven't the right," Lush continued, as if the younger man hadn't spoken, "but I can still haul you to the woodshed if I have to, and you're surely pushing my patience."

The deputy cocked his head to one side and squinted.

Lush breathed a heavy sigh. "I'm your papa, you cast-iron idiot, come back from twenty years of booz-ing and wild times with his tail betwixt his legs! I might be coming back with a different name and a grizzled beard, and I wouldn't blame you if you were mad enough or bitter enough to put a slug through my heart right here and now, but what this young lady's telling you is the truth. You'd best listen to her."

Clementine was flabbergasted. She hadn't realized that the old trapper had that many words in him. It was practically an oration!

The deputy was shocked, too, but for an entirely different reason. He stood there, stammering, trying to peer through all the dirt and hair and time on Lush's face. "My papa's dead," he said finally. "Mama said so."

"Well, Pansy *would* say that, wouldn't she?" Lush snapped right back. He looked vaguely disgusted. "It'd be just like the old witch. Always was more concerned about what the neighbors might be thinking than the truth of anything. Honestly, Josh. Will you either holster that gun or use it?"

The boy blinked rapidly. "How . . . how'd you know my name?"

"Aren't you listening, son?" Lush asked. To Clementine, he suddenly seemed about two inches taller. "I'm your father, that's how," he went on. "I know your name's Joshua Cornwall Simpson, and that you were born to Mary and Yarnell Simpson on May the seventh, eighteen and thirty-six, in a cabin alongside the Chickasaw Creek in Cutler County, Virginia, and that you've got a strawberry birthmark on your right butt cheek. Least, you still had it when you were four."

"Yarnell?" said Clementine.

Lush paused to turn toward her, and said, "Yes'm. And I hope you'll be forgivin' my hard language."

She nodded dumbly.

"I heard two years back that there was a Josh Simpson, 'bout the right age, doing part-time deputying here in Jupiter. I've worked myself all the way down from Colorado, just to see if it was my boy Josh," Lush said, then nodded crisply. "It is. You're the spitting image of my pappy. Well," he admitted, tilting his head, "you do have your mama's chin . . ."

Deputy Josh Simpson blanched and collapsed back on the edge of the desk. Clementine couldn't say that she blamed him.

"Pa?" he said weakly. "You ain't dead? A bear didn't get you?"

Lush came forward and rested his hand on the deputy's shoulder. To Clementine, he said, "If you've got business to take care of for Fargo, you'd best be getting to it. My boy and I will be putting together a rescue party. Won't we, Josh?"

Deputy Simpson nodded dully.

Zeb Daggett was halfway down the mountain when the pains came over him again.

He tried to stay in the saddle. He clung to the horn like a wood tick, but the pain was burning like a matchhead in his chest and finally, he slid from the saddle.

Sounds came through the pain, sounds of horses being reined up, of boots tramping through brush, and then voices, all jumbled up.

"Get back, dammit! Give him some air!"

He recognized the voice as Luke Shepherd's, his foreman.

"Mr. Daggett?" he said, genuine distress in his voice. Daggett was oddly comforted to hear it. "Mr. Daggett? Can you hear me?"

He nodded, still grimacing with the pain. It was leaving him, but more slowly than before. Each time, it was worse and lasted longer.

"Harley," Shepherd barked, his head turned, "get me that canteen off'a there."

"I'm all right," Daggett managed, although just that much was a struggle.

Shepherd held the canteen to his lips, and Daggett took a sip of water.

Shepherd said, "You boys cut some pine saplings and rig together a travois for Mr. Daggett. We'll take him back up the—"

"No," said Daggett. He propped himself up on one elbow. "I can ride."

Shepherd bent close and whispered, "Are you sure, Mr. Daggett? You're white as milk and still shakin'. I'd a lot rather see you back up to the ranch house, lyin' down in your own bed."

Daggett sat all the way up. He was still dizzy, but the worst of the pain had subsided. He rubbed at his still-throbbing arm. "We're not going back to the ranch," he said.

"But, Mr. Daggett—"

"Don't 'but' me, Mr. Shepherd," he said with more anger than he intended. After all, it wasn't any of Shepherd's doing that he was an old man, failing at last and fighting it every inch of the way.

He rested a hand on Shepherd's arm. "Sorry," he said. "Not your fault."

Shepherd said, "I'd feel a lot better if Doc Martin had a look at you."

"That bumbling quack!" Daggett spat. "Nothing but a drunk."

Above him, one of the men—Harley, he thought—said, "You still want us to rig up that travois, Shepherd?"

Daggett answered for him. "No, goddamnit. Help me up."

Shepherd aided him to his feet, and then to his horse. "Wish you'd reconsider, boss," he said as he helped Daggett into the saddle.

Daggett gathered his reins. The pain was almost a memory now, except for a lingering tightness in his chest. He looked around at the thinning trees. They'd be out of the mountains and down into the foothills within an hour, and down to the spring—and the mine—in less than two hours more, if they pushed.

At this moment, he wanted nothing so much as to see this fabled mine of Tucker's, to touch walls that old Spanish picks had chiseled from living rock, and to see this horde of silver. He wanted to sashay into the claims office, big as life, and register a claim on land everybody thought was his already. Now, that would be a laugh!

"Mount up, Mr. Shepherd," he said. "We've still got some hard trail ahead of us."

# 16

Stripped to the waist, slick with sweat, and staggering beneath his burden, Fargo reached the pile of rubble he'd already wrestled out of the tunnel and with a grunt, heaved the rock he carried to the top. Like the last few, it refused to stay put, and tumbled down the side.

He was building a whole new mountain out here, he thought, and for not the first time since he and Weasel had started that morning. The pile, which had been a goodly heap last night, now stretched out into three mammoth mounds, the first two chest-high and at least fifteen feet around.

But they'd managed to tunnel back to where they'd been when the second cave-in had struck, and maybe a few feet beyond. Some boulders had proved too massive for even the two of them together to budge, and they'd left them where they lay. Now the excavation included climbing over and around them on each trip in and out.

He had dragged out countless blankets, laden with pebbles and dirt, too, but most of the time, he didn't bother. When the loose dirt and gravel proved too deep and too slippery, they'd just kick a path through it. In places, the walls of the tunnel had two-feet-high drifts of small stones, pebbles, and rocks up to the size of small watermelons.

He slumped down in the shade of the end pile,

opened his canteen and took a long drink, then held the canteen up and let the rest of the water cascade down over his head and shoulders. They ached, not just from the labor, but because the tunnel ceiling was so low. He had to bend just to travel through it, and each time, he was bending while carrying a hundred pounds of rock, or better.

It was miserable work, made no less palatable by the men he was tunneling to save.

If they were still alive.

Weasel emerged then, also stripped to the waist and looking just as grimy with grit and dust as Fargo figured he himself did. Weasel was a strange sight, though. His torso and arms, long hidden from the sun's rays by cloth and hide, were almost ghostly pale beneath the grime as was his forehead, which, Fargo supposed, was always covered by his floppy hat.

If he had held Weasel down and given him a shave, Fargo reckoned that he'd look just like a racoon, the only band of tan on his body being the strip over his eyes and nose.

"By Gawd, Fargo!" Weasel announced as he slumped to the ground and closed his eyes. "The Good Lord weren't foolin' when he made rocks heavy. That's for dang sure!" The work was taking its toll on the old trapper. That was the first thing he'd said in over an hour, and weariness had cut deep circles under his eyes.

"Mean work," said Fargo. It was all he could manage.

"Yup," replied Weasel

They sat there in silence for a time, then Fargo stood again. "Hungry?"

Weasel nodded. "Reckon."

"Got some jerky in my pack," he said, walking down toward the supplies. "No time for cooking." He looked up at the sun. It was eleven o'clock, or thereabouts. Clementine and Lush ought to be bringing a rescue party within an hour. Maybe less.

Maybe a lot more, if that dithering excuse for a deputy got snarly on them.

He pulled the packet of jerky free of his pack and took a hunk, then carried another to Weasel, along with a fresh canteen.

Weasel took both gratefully, gnawing off a bit of the dried meat before he opened the canteen and took three big, rapid gulps. Water trickled down his beard and cut clean furrows through the dust on the white, wrinkled skin of his chest, on which sprouted exactly four long, straight hairs, all grizzled.

"How'd you come to start that?" Fargo asked as he chewed.

"What?" Weasel asked, intent on his jerky.

"Braiding your beard," Fargo said. "Don't believe I ever saw that before. Well, I knew a fellow up in Oregon that braided his mustache ends. Course that was because he was too cheap to buy the wax. But I don't believe I ever knew anybody to plait a whole beard before."

Weasel winked, and dug a finger into his cheek to scratch. "Well, I reckon it just got to be a habit. Got snowed in up to the San Francisco Peaks 'bout three year back. Wintered in an old lean-to some feller had built. He must'a been a right fussy sort, 'cause he had a piece of broken mirror stashed in there, all propped up on a shelf in the corner. Edge of it weren't broke good enough to shave with, so I started in to braidin' one night to pass the time."

Weasel gave out with an ornery grin, and gnawed a thick string off his jerky with his big yellow teeth. "A red-headed whore admired me when I got out in the spring," he said, still smiling, "so I jus' kept on a'braidin' it."

Fargo chuckled. "Good a reason as any. Was Lush with you?"

Weasel washed down the jerky with another gulp of water. "Nope. I was all on my lonesome. Lush and me partnered up the next year. To hear him tell it, he was a wild'un up till then. A lot of drinkin' and rowdy-dowin'.."

"What?" said Fargo, half-teasing. "This the same Lush you're riding with now? The quiet little hombre in the coonskin cap?"

"The self-same," Weasel replied, " 'cept he ain't so quiet. You ain't wintered with him." He stood and stretched his sinewy arms. "Well, I reckon we best get our backsides back to diggin'. Grab up that lantern and bring your carcass down the tunnel with me, 'cause I needs you to help me wedge this ol' timber into place and shore up the roof. Dang thing's gonna come down on me, otherwise. Might anyway. Wood's so old it's about rotted through."

They picked up their lanterns, and Fargo followed him down the tunnel.

"What do mean, you haven't rounded up anybody yet?" Clementine demanded. She was back from her errand, the precious paper in her pocket, and now she wanted nothing more than to climb on that Ovaro and fan him west, back to Fargo.

But Deputy Simpson just stood there, looking sheepish. "Well, I guess Sheriff Tucker wasn't as well-liked as I thought, miss," he said. "I been over to all three saloons, and what few fellers there was just shrugged their shoulders. I ain't even told 'em why Tucker and Reeves was out there. I mean, about what Pa told me they done. I'm sure sorry, miss. About your daddy and uncle, I mean."

Well, he was calling Lush "Pa," now. She suspected it was a step in the right direction, but it wasn't getting men to the cave-in any faster. It crossed her mind that with the law being sort of on their side now, Fargo wouldn't have to worry about being hauled in on a trumped-up charge. And for just a second, she considered that it didn't really matter anymore.

But then, the better part of herself took hold.

"Deputy, may I remind you that there are men down there? Living, breathing men. At least, I hope they still are."

"I realize that, miss, but—"

"Call me Clementine."

"Yes'm. But I don't think that Pa and me'll be enough to do it, and I can't get nobody churned up to go out there."

She looked around. "Where is Mr. Fillpot—I mean, your pa—now?"

"Down to Ezra's barberin' shop, gettin' a shave. I told him I reckoned there'd be time."

Clementine ground her teeth. Of all the time to trim a beard! She must have walked right past him, too!

"Come on, Deputy," she said, and snagging his sleeve, headed down the street toward the first saloon.

"You can call me Josh," he said, stumbling behind her.

"Speed up, Josh," she said, and pulled him through the swinging doors of the Red Dog Saloon.

There were a total of five men in the place, including the barkeep, but five would be enough.

"Gentlemen!" she announced.

One head, sporting a heavy, handlebar mustache, turned lazily toward her, then took in Deputy Simpson. "If this is about that dog Tucker and his no-account buddy, Reeves, you can just go on down the street." He turned around again.

"Good riddance to bad rubbish," said another man.

A third agreed with him.

"See?" said Deputy Simpson, with a shrug of his shoulders.

Clementine muttered something nasty about men in general, and then walked forward, to the center of the room. "Gentlemen?"

Not one head came up.

"Gentlemen, may I please have your attention!"

Only the man with the handlebar mustache looked up, and then only grudgingly. The rest kept their noses buried in their cards, probably wishing she'd go away and quit making them feel guilty.

There had been a time when she'd walked into a room and every head had turned. Not today. Today, she was filthy and wild-haired and wearing men's clothing to boot. Not much of a head turner. But then she smiled. She had something they'd look at, all right.

With no further adieu, she unbuttoned her shirt and held the halves of it wide.

From the corner of her eye, she saw Deputy Simpson stagger against a table and fall into a chair.

The owner of the handlebar mustache said, "Jesus H!" just before his jaw dropped.

One by one they looked up. She supposed these boys didn't get out much. One of them kept swallowing repeatedly, his Adam's apple bouncing up and down in his throat like a rubber ball, and another dropped his beer mug on the floor. When it shattered, nobody moved so much as a muscle.

She waited until every mother's son of them was staring at her, gap-mouthed and nearly drooling, and then she smiled and covered herself.

Hugging the sides of her shirt around her, she said, "Do I have everybody's attention now?"

One man, who was still staring at her chest—for all the good it did him—nodded slowly.

"Do all you fellows have horses?"

They all nodded slowly.

"Good," she said. "Now, what we're going to do is all mount up and ride west, and help to dig out your Sheriff Tucker and that bastard Deputy Reeves."

They just kept staring at her chest.

Her brow creased. "Boys?" she said, in a sterner tone.

"Yes'm," ventured one cowpoke at the back. "Whatever you say, ma'am. Miss."

"*Now*, boys," she said, and chairs started scraping.

As they filed slowly past her, she heard the man in the handlebar mustache ask the fellow next to him, "Why're we going out there?"

The other fellow hissed, "Guess we're gonna dig 'em up after all. And shut up, Mike. Maybe she'll do it again."

The man in the handlebar mustache gulped. "Shit. You think?"

When the men were all outside the saloon and mounted up, Clementine turned to Josh Simpson.

"We'd better get Mr. Fillpot and get our behinds moving, Josh," she said. When she received no answer, she looked up.

"Lawd," he whispered. "I never seen the like! I thought Blond Alice, up the street, had her a mighty impressive pair of—"

"Josh?" she interjected. "My face is up here."

He met her eyes, flushed beet red, then looked at his feet. And then he brightened. "Are we . . . are we goin' down the street to the next saloon?"

"Oh, for heaven's sake," she muttered, then brushed past him. "These men are enough, and besides, I don't want to give them time to think about it and change their minds. C'mon, get your hind end up out of that chair and let's just go! There are men dying out there, men who should be taking up space in the prison at Yuma."

She burst out onto the sidewalk to find her five men—including the bartender—now waiting mutely on horseback.

"Follow me," she said, and with Josh Simpson close on her heels, she set out up the street at a jog, headed for the sheriff's office and Fargo's Ovaro. The others trotted after her like sheep after a belled ewe.

When, panting slightly, she reached the office, there

was a man sitting atop Lush Fillpot's horse, a stranger wearing stiff new dungarees and a store-bought plaid shirt with the price tag still hanging from the collar. Bits of bloody tissue paper still clung to his too-white, fresh-shaved cheeks and throat, and the back of his neck was pale as parchment where the long hair had been barbered away.

Clementine stopped stock-still.

"Mr. Fillpot?" she said, blinking.

"Yes, ma'am," came the answer from that rather distinguished, although still shy, face. It was scrubbed clean, too, and surprisingly handsome. He cleared his throat. "Hadn't we better, uh . . ."

"You're right, Mr. Fillpot," she said, and climbed onto the Ovaro's back. There was no time to waste. "We better had."

Beside her, Josh Simpson swung a leg over his bay. "Pa?" he said, his face working overtime. "Is that you?"

Lush reined his horse away from the rail. "Yes, son," he said stoically, "it is."

Josh shook his head. "Jeez, Pa! Would you mind stayin' the same for a little while, so's I can get used to you?"

"There'll be time to talk on the trail," Clementine said, then turned toward the other riders. "Ready, boys?"

They nodded, as one.

She urged the Ovaro into a canter.

# 17

In the black depths of the cave, Reeves had become certain he was going mad. He'd forgotten about water—how greenhorn stupid, to live in a desert and not think about water!—but he was surely thinking about it now.

He ran his swollen tongue over cracked lips. Why couldn't the rockslide have trapped him in that big cave, the one with the water? No, that water was likely bad, poisoned from sitting there for about a million years. It'd probably kill him in minutes.

It wasn't a bad idea.

He'd begun to hear things, there in the dark. He'd heard his little sister's voice, clear as a bell. What she said didn't make any sense, but it was her voice, all right. For a minute he'd thought she was right there beside him, dressed in crinolines and ribbons and holding that stupid doll of hers and shaking a pudgy finger at him.

*I'm gonna tell, Clay! I'm gonna tell on you!*

Now, that was funny! The last time he'd seen Gladys, she was all grown up, not a little girl anymore, and she was fat and greasy-aproned and mean as a pit viper.

And bells, he kept hearing bells. Not big church bells, but those little silvery ones, like his mother used to hang on the tree at Christmas. They didn't really ring so much as they clapped. He remembered Pa coming home drunk that one Christmas Eve and falling into it, lit candles, bells, and all.

It had burnt the whole damn house down, and they had to spend Christmas Day—and the remainder of the winter, too, for that matter—huddling for warmth in the tool shed.

"Don't go gettin' maudlin on me, Reeves," said Tucker, clear as day.

"Shut up," Reeves rasped, shivering. "You're dead. I killed you."

"You're not gonna get rid of me that easy, boy."

Reeves picked up a rock from the ore pile and threw it blindly. It hit something soft.

"Sticks and stones," said the sheriff's voice from the darkness. "Sticks and stones."

Reeves began to weep.

Luke Shepherd, Daggett's foreman, lay atop the rise from which Fargo had spied on the Apaches. Now Shepherd was doing the same, except what he saw was two white men: one old, one in his prime. They were both stripped to the waist and shiny with sweat, and were busily hauling rocks out into the open from a man-made cleft in the hillside.

They must have been working at it a long time, because the piles of debris they were building out by the spring were impressive.

He'd seen the old man only one time, but the younger one came in and out repeatedly, tottering under the weight of a new stone each time. He paused now and again to steal a gulp from a canteen or to mop his brow before he headed down the shaft again.

Although Shepherd had thought at first that it was the sheriff and one of his deputies down there, stealing Daggett's silver, he recognized neither one of them as Farley Tucker. He'd met the sheriff twice, and neither one of these gents was short or burly enough to be him.

Daggett had told him the bare bones of the story, about how the sheriff was supposed to run a couple of claim jumpers off his land who'd supposedly found the lost Santa Rosa mine. He had his doubts about that last part—the Santa Rosa was a campfire legend, nothing more—but it sure didn't appear to him that Tucker had run anybody off.

Shepherd lowered his spyglass, tucked it carefully into its case, and thumbed back his hat. To be honest, even though Daggett had told him flat out that he owned this land, Shepherd thought otherwise. He knew Daggett's spread better than anybody else—Daggett included, lately—and for the life of him, he didn't remember the Inca Land and Cattle Company's holdings going this far south. Now and then their cattle wandered down this far south or farther, and every once in a while they lost a few of those wandering steers to some half-starved Apache.

He remembered Daggett telling him that just this last winter. To just write it off as a loss. That what cattle that had wandered off Inca Land and Cattle Company land were fair game for the Indians, if the hands didn't find them first.

But now Daggett was firm in his conviction that he was being robbed blind—and of the find of the century at that!

By the looks of those men down by the spring and what they were toting, Daggett wasn't being robbed of anything but rocks and a whole lot of sweat.

He didn't know whose land this was, but it wasn't Daggett's.

Still, Daggett was the boss. He was ornery and overly formal and sometimes he could be mean as a sack of badgers, but underneath it he was a good man, a fair man, and he paid Shepherd's wages. He was sick, too, so sick that Shepherd had been fretting about it, off and on, for the past few months.

The damned old buzzard wouldn't admit a thing, of

course, and wouldn't see the doctor, either. He supposed Daggett would figure that would be tantamount to giving in to the sickness, as if admitting it existed was bowing to it.

Shepherd slid down the slope and mounted his horse. He'd have to tell him that those miners were still there.

He didn't like giving Daggett bad news.

It was the old man's heart, of course. Shepherd had seen his own father act much the same way before the end came. The stabbing chest pains, the shortness of breath, even the way he grabbed at his arm. Daggett tried to hide it, but Shepherd had seen him taken with it twice before today's episode. It had gotten so that he rarely told Daggett anything upsetting that happened on the ranch, for fear it would bring on a new attack.

Well, he couldn't help bringing him this news, although it wasn't the news itself that he feared would bring on another episode. It was what he was afraid Daggett would order them to do next. Daggett would be dead, sooner or later, but the rest of them would have to live with it for the rest of their lives.

A frown deepening the lines of his face, he started back to meet Daggett and the others at a slow walk. No sense in hurrying the inevitable.

"Be careful!" Fargo hissed when a rock nearly crushed his foot.

Weasel just looked at it, then up at Fargo. He shrugged. "I tosses 'em, you catches 'em," he said crabbily. "That's the way she works."

Fargo leaned wearily against the wall of the tunnel, only to feel a sharp edge of raw stone digging into his back. He stood up again into what was becoming his characteristic slouch. The only place he could stand up was a stretch of the tunnel about fifteen feet long, where the roof had caved in to such a degree that it was probably a good twenty feet overhead.

That's where all the damn rocks had come from. He and Weasel had tried to shore it up with the rotting timbers they'd dug from beneath the fall of stone, but the timbers had been too brittle and the ceiling far too high.

"Well, look before you toss, dammit!" Fargo snarled.

Weasel shoved another rock into his arms, and it was so heavy it nearly took him to the floor.

They were both getting grouchy, Fargo thought as he struggled down the tunnel. They'd dug and carried and carried and dug, and then, with only three hours of sleep, had dug and carried again for another eight or nine hours without a break.

They were building their fourth heap of rocks, now. Pretty soon they'd have a wide fence of rocks piled nearly up to the mouth of the tunnel. And he'd like nothing more than to drop down into the cool, purple shade of that fence and sleep and sleep and sleep, and then wake up and find Clementine there beside him.

Naked, if possible.

He sighed, and wiped a sheen of sweat from his face with the flat of his hand. No rest for the wicked. And Clementine should be there with a rescue party anytime now.

He looked to the east, as he had every time he'd hauled another rock outside for the last hour. Still no cloud of dust to announce approaching riders. What was keeping her, anyway?

He was about to duck back inside the tunnel again, to see what tortuous new burden Weasel had chosen for him, when he heard a small sound—distant, but out of place. He froze.

Turning slowly, as if to get his canteen again, he flicked his eyes up and cast a quick, sweeping glance to the north.

He caught a glimpse of color, of something that

shouldn't be there. He bent toward his canteen, but instead, snagged his gunbelt and slowly backed toward the tunnel. If it was Apaches again—and especially, if they were the sort of Apaches who didn't bother to parley—he was going to be ready for them.

He had just reached the entrance when a shot sang off the rock beside him. He felt shards of rock bite sharply into his cheek before he heard the report. Cursing, he scrambled back into the gloom.

Whoever was out there, red or white, they weren't friendly. Not by a long shot.

# 18

"Who fired that rifle?" Daggett barked, and Shepherd cringed.

Down the line of Daggett's men, secreted by the roll of the desert, a young man, no more than twenty, stepped back from the rise and held up his gun. "I did, sir!"

"Well, stop it," Daggett said. It came out weak, and he motioned to Shepherd.

Shepherd called, "Hold your damn fire, Jim!" and then turned back to his employer. "You look bad again, Mr. Daggett. Do you want—"

Daggett jerked away from the hand Shepherd had placed on his shoulder. "I'm fine," he said through clenched teeth, but Shepherd knew the pains were back. "Why did that fool start shooting, anyway? I wanted to get closer and talk to those boys down there before anybody got gun happy."

"Everybody's pretty tense, sir," Shepherd said.

He didn't add that it was Daggett making them edgy. They all knew there was something wrong. Even the meanest, orneriest hand had a soft spot for old Zebulon Daggett—even poor, dumb Jim Crowley, who had actually fired—and wanted to take out his anger and frustration on the nearest possible target, which just happened to be those poor miners down there.

"Jim saw that fellow pick up his gunbelt," Shepherd explained. "I guess he thought—"

Daggett waved a hand, stopping him. "What he thought's neither here nor there."

The pain must have stopped, because color was seeping back into the old man's cheeks. Not much, but enough that Shepherd relaxed a little.

Daggett, too, seemed less edgy. "All right," he said. "Let's get closer. Tell the men to get down to that little rise, but stay in back of it. And no shooting. Then you and I and Harley Jakes will raise a white flag and go down there, and hope to hell we don't get shot. I want to keep this as peaceable as possible."

"Right." Shepherd touched his hat, then jogged down the line and gathered the men about him. He gave out instructions quickly, and the men began leading their mounts away, behind the cover of the gently rising and falling land. Jim Crowley, however, lagged behind.

"Would you tell Mr. Daggett I'm right sorry?" he said meekly. He was a big boy, soft-faced and a little pudgy through the middle despite plenty of hard work. Daggett fed his men well, and Jim took advantage of it. He'd come to work for Daggett at the age of sixteen, after the death of his parents over near Santa Fe. Right now, it looked like it wouldn't take much of a nudge to push him to tears.

"It's all right, son," Shepherd said. "Mr. Daggett understands how jumpy you boys are. He's jumpy, too. Now get with the others, and put that long gun back in its sheath."

He'd said it with a grin, and Jim smiled back at him. Sliding his rifle into the boot on his saddle, he took off, leading his horse at a good clip to catch up with the others.

Harley was waiting nearby, as he'd been told. "What now?" he asked, and spat out a brown stream of tobacco juice.

Shepherd thumbed back his hat. "Don't suppose you've got anything white on you?"

Harley scowled. "What the hell for?"

"Truce flag."

"Christ. Next thing you know," he muttered as he dug into his saddlebag and felt around, "we'll be askin' 'em up to the ranch house for tea an' cookies." He came up with something wadded into a ball and decidedly dingy gray, and waved it. "Got my spare socks."

"I said, white."

"Well, they *was* white, once upon a time!" Harley growled defensively.

Shepherd sighed. "Never mind. We'll find something."

"Why in tarnation didn't you bring my rifle, too!" Weasel ranted. He kept his voice down to prevent another cave-in, but if they'd been outside, Fargo was sure he would have been treated to an eardrum-shattering tirade.

"I already told you," Fargo said, and wiped fresh blood from his cheek. He was peeking around the bend in the tunnel, and there was still no sign of the men who had shot at him. Fatigue tore at every part of his body, but his mind was on alert. The peppering his face had taken had seen to that.

"Well," Weasel began again, "you just explain to me how the devil I'm supposed to—"

Fargo wheeled toward him. "Shut *up!*" he snapped.

Weasel jerked his head back so fast that he hit it on the roof of the tunnel. Rubbing his skull, he grimaced and whispered, "Well, you don't need to go gettin' so all-fired snippy about it. I was just askin', that's all."

Muttering under his breath, Fargo turned his attention back toward the shaft in front of him, toward the far-away window on the world that its mouth provided.

Still he saw nothing.

"You reckon they went away?" Weasel asked, his eyebrows working.

"No."

"Well, where you reckon they are?"

Fargo closed his eyes and swore to himself. If Weasel didn't watch out, he was going to find himself knocked cold for the duration.

"I don't know, Weasel," he said. "You can see just as good as I can."

"Hell, I can't see a damn thing!" Weasel complained next to his ear. "You're taking up the whole gull-durn view! The part that's safe, leastwise."

"Fine," Fargo hissed, and moved back, taking a few steps down the tunnel, toward the cave-in. "You keep watch. They don't seem real anxious to get to us."

Weasel moved forward to Fargo's previous position. "I'm real thankful for your vote'a confidence," he remarked snidely.

Fargo didn't answer. He supposed the combination of too much work and too little sleep was pulling Weasel's strings, too.

Instead, he said, "I doubt they'll make a move very soon. I'm going to go back and take a listen. If you did hear something, if the sound can get out, maybe air can get back there, too."

"Told you I weren't sure," Weasel said, still keen on the desert outside. "Maybe it was them Spanish ghosts singin'. Didn't hear but a snatch." He paused. "I got half a mind to just walk out there. Maybe it were a stray slug. Maybe somebody was huntin'."

Fargo didn't say anything.

"Oh, all right," grumbled Weasel. "Leave me your gun."

"No."

"Why the hell not?"

Again, Fargo remained silent.

Weasel looked up at the roof of the tunnel, and then said, "Oh. Well, hurry up an' check, then. If them fellers come for us, I s'pose I can beat 'em to death with a rock. Got plenty'a those."

Fargo turned and started down the tunnel, angling this way and that around boulders, ducking low, then standing erect where the ceiling permitted. It wasn't the best time take a run down the tunnel, but if anybody was alive in there, he had to make sure they were getting enough air to keep them that way.

He reached the edge of the rockfall with some difficulty, and pressed his ear against it. And heard absolutely nothing.

Maybe Weasel was right, that it was the dead Spaniards that had come back to whisper to an old man.

He was just about to take his ear away and go back up front, when he thought he heard something. He waited.

There it was again. It was very faint, so faint that the sound of the blood beating in his ears all but obscured it. But it was there, all right, a voice singing an old sailing song.

He recognized the tune, and the snatches of scratchy words he made out: " 'Shave his belly with a rusty razor, shave his belly with a rusty razor, shave his belly with a rusty razor, early in the morning . . .' "

Fargo lifted his head from the rock. It seemed they were about to rescue Long John Silver. Well, any man who could sing that loud and that long had plenty of air. He could wait.

He was just starting up the tunnel again, weaving around the lanterns Weasel had set out at intervals and the boulders they hadn't been able to budge, when Weasel came scuttling toward him, head down and barreling along the shaft like the red-eyed hounds of hell were on his tail.

"Give me your gun, damn it!" he roared.

123

"Quiet!" Fargo hissed at the same instant that two quick shots rang out.

Weasel's momentum carried him forward even as the roar of the amplified gunshots rang in Fargo's ears. He crashed into Fargo just as the earth began to tremble and groan and the air filled with dust.

The rocks came next.

He dragged Weasel deeper into the tunnel, away from the crashing stones that rained down between them and the only exit. He scrambled over rocks, half tripped and took the skin off his back on a rough boulder as more rocks pelted down. And always, he pulled Weasel along with him.

And then he was in the clear and there was darkness, alleviated only by the single lantern that had survived, the lantern beside the rockfall to which he'd pressed his ear and heard life. Behind them and in front, floor to ceiling, there was a solid wall of rocky debris.

The air was thick with dust, so thick that Fargo could barely breathe. He reached into his back pocket and pulled free a bandanna, and quickly tied it over his nose and mouth. Still choking, he turned to Weasel.

The old man lay crumpled beside him, and when Fargo eased him onto his side, he saw the hole the slug had ripped in him. It was high in his back, high enough that it had probably missed anything vital, and Fargo breathed out a sigh of relief.

He wasn't comforted for more than a second, though. Whoever had shot Weasel wasn't somebody he'd trust to dig them out.

Still fighting the dust, he moved Weasel to a more comfortable position and dug through his pockets until he found a handkerchief, which he tied over Weasel's nose and mouth. The old trapper would live through the shooting, but Fargo didn't want to lose him to asphyxiation.

And then he slumped down. His scraped back stung

angrily when he leaned against the rock, and his hip and leg smarted where they had been dealt glancing blows by falling rocks. He shifted his weight so that he was at least halfway comfortable, and let his head loll back against the stones.

Through them, he heard someone singing, just faintly, " 'What do you do with a drunken sailor, what do you do with a drunken sailor . . .' "

He sat forward, so that he couldn't hear it anymore.

"Clementine," he whispered, "where the hell are you?"

# 19

"I swear, Mr. Shepherd, there was somethin' in his hand!" McCafferty said indignantly, and for the third time. "Could've been a gun, so I shot at him a couple times. And ain't no way I'm gonna apologize for defendin' myself."

Shepherd was too angry to debate it with him. Through clenched teeth, he said, "You're fired, McCafferty," and tearing a worn leather wallet from his back pocket, pulled out seventeen dollars and handed it to the man.

"That'll take care of your back pay," he said. "Now get out." Without another word, he turned his back on the stunned McCafferty and bent over to Daggett.

Daggett hadn't even made it as far as the spring, the poor son of a bitch. He'd folded up halfway there, then insisted that three men go down to the mine anyway, carrying a flag of truce. Shepherd had chosen to stay with his fallen employer, and sent Harley, young Jim, and McCafferty.

He hadn't realized that McCafferty was so damned jumpy. Now the fool had buried those two poor miners alive.

"Mr. Daggett?" he said, bending close. They'd carried him to the edge of the spring, and he now lay, pale and drawn, in the thin, blue-gray shade of a paloverde. "Can you hear me, sir?"

Daggett's lips moved, but no sound came out.

Jim appeared on the other side of Daggett, bearing fresh water. His face nearly as white as Daggett's, he knelt and handed the canteen to Shepherd.

"Is he . . . is he gonna . . . ?"

"It's all right, Jim," Shepherd soothed, although the words sounded hollow, even to him. "Thanks for the water." Gently, he raised Daggett's head and held the canteen to his lips. Daggett took a few weak sips, but most of it ran down his chin and soaked a dark line into his collar.

He whispered something.

Shepherd leaned down. He put his ear close.

Daggett whispered something again.

"Paper?" said Shepherd. "You want paper and a pen?" He looked over at Jim and shook his head.

Jim swallowed. "I . . . I got my Bible in my pack. Would that do? And a lead stub I was usin' to keep count of the steers last week." He blushed. "I never can get the hang of that thing you fellas do with the knots in the cord."

Daggett gave a stuttery nod, and Shepherd said, "I reckon that'd do just fine, Jim. You run and get 'em."

His eyes still closed, Daggett whispered, "Good lad."

"Yes," said Shepherd. "He is. You hurt much, boss?"

"Not so much now," Daggett whispered with some difficulty. "Tired. You . . . did you . . . the mine . . ."

Shepherd knew what he was trying to say. "I've got the men digging their way back to 'em," he said. "I don't have much hope that they're alive, though."

Daggett squeezed his hand, just a little. "Always hope," he breathed.

Shepherd turned his head toward the mouth of the tunnel. Men dragged small stones and gravel from the shaft in blankets and lugged big rocks by hand to the huge pile the miners had begun. He glanced east, and saw the last of McCafferty's dust disappearing toward Jupiter. He frowned. Stupid bastard.

Jim had returned, and knelt down again. He handed the worn Bible and his lead stub to Shepherd.

"Sir?" said Shepherd. "Jim's brought the Bible and the lead."

Daggett opened his eyes to slits. "Good boy, Jim. Stay put." He swallowed again, and signaled for more water, which Shepherd gave him.

"All right," the old man said after he swallowed. "Write what I say."

Deep in the belly of the hill, the dust had settled. Weasel was slumped on the floor in a place Fargo had cleared of stones, and was still out cold.

He'd turned the lantern down low to conserve air, but before he had, he'd found a canteen that was nearly full. Weasel must have brought it down the shaft without Fargo having noticed.

He took the bandanna off his face and blew what seemed like a pound of dust and grit out of his nose, then took a short drink to settle the dust clogging his throat. He replaced the canteen's cap carefully. No telling how long it would have to last.

The singing from beyond the wall of stones had stopped. That was a mercy. Fargo figured he had two choices—to start tunneling out, or keep tunneling inward. Well, three choices, really—he could always just sit on his ass and wait for something to happen, but that wasn't in the Trailsman's nature.

He dug in his back pocket, wincing hard at the sharp sting in his back, and pulled out a coin.

"Heads, I start digging to the outside," he said, tossing it in the air. "Tails, back to the cave." He caught it and slapped it down on his wrist.

He held his hands to the lantern, then peered between them, at the coin.

Tails.

128

"Figures," he muttered.

Slowly, with his leg and hip throbbing, his head pounding, and his back stinging like a thousand angry wasps, he pulled himself up into that now too-familiar crouch.

He started moving rocks.

Clementine had just signaled the men to slow their mounts and rest them for the final time when she saw the rider headed toward them.

At first she felt a profound sense of joy, a lightness at the thought that it might be Fargo, coming to tell her that they'd got to the men and that everything was all right. But then she realized how foolish this was. The two men couldn't have dug their way back to the cave by now just themselves. And even if they had managed it, she was certain both men would simply collapse out of sheer exhaustion the moment the job was completed.

Mr. Fillpot—or should she say, Mr. Simpson—had dismounted and was walking his horse alongside the Ovaro. "Fellow seems to be in a hurry," he commented as the rider drew near.

It was true. The rider didn't slow until he was almost upon them. Even then, it appeared as if he was going to veer around them, except that the man in the handlebar mustache—whose name, she had learned, was Mike Hoskins—shouted, "Hey! McCafferty!" just before the man reached them.

He reined in. His horse was lathered and blowing hard, and stood with his head down and his sides heaving.

McCafferty, however, paid it no heed. He leaned on his saddle horn, and said, "What you doin' out here, Mike?"

"Treatin' my horse a good bit better'n you, by the looks of it," Mike replied.

McCafferty frowned. "I'll walk him in a bit. What's

it to you? And what're you fellers doing out in the middle of nowhere, anyhow?" Just then he looked at Clementine, and his eyes lit up. "What you doin' draggin' that female in boy's clothes along? Blond Alice get replaced by new blood?"

"We're a rescue party, Mr. McCafferty," Clementine spoke up, and none too gently. She didn't know exactly who Blond Alice might be, but considering the girl's name, she had a fair notion. Additionally, she didn't care one whit for McCafferty's tone.

"We're goin' to the old Santa Rosa mine," Deputy Simpson added. "Sheriff Tucker and Deputy Reeves are trapped out there. They had a cave-in. There's two fellers out there now, diggin' for 'em, and Clementine, here, came to town for help."

McCafferty, who hadn't taken his eyes off her, said, "Did she, now?"

"Yup," replied Deputy Simpson. "She's the only one of us what knows where the dang thing is."

Clementine started leading the Ovaro forward again. "You're welcome to come and help, Mr. McCafferty, but we've no time to stand and pass the time of day with you."

The others started forward, too, passing McCafferty as he called, "Snippy little piece, ain't she?"

She heard the voices—though not the words—of men back in the line, and then laughter.

Clementine was too tired to be embarrassed. She just kept trudging. Let them talk about her. She'd gotten their attention hadn't she? They were on their way to help Fargo dig, weren't they? That was all that mattered now.

Behind her, she heard McCafferty give a last, rough laugh, and then she heard him push that poor, winded horse into a canter again. Its hoofbeats vanished into the desert behind them.

"Moron," she muttered under her breath.

"Funny, McCafferty bein' out here all by his lonesome," Deputy Simpson said.

She ducked her head beneath the Ovaro's powerful neck to peer at him. "Why's that, Josh?"

He shrugged. "Last I heard, he was workin' for Old Man Daggett, up at his place. Just think it's funny he'd be this far south, that's all."

A sudden chill gripped Clementine. McCafferty had come directly from the mine, nearly on the path she'd taken to get to town. If Daggett was at the mine—Daggett, the man who'd told Sheriff Tucker to get rid of her father and uncle—she doubted he'd be any more opened-minded with Fargo and Weasel.

And then she realized that McCafferty hadn't seemed the least bit surprised at the mention of the Santa Rosa. He hadn't even seemed curious.

She was fully awake now, no longer the walking dead leading a plodding horse through the desert.

Fargo was in trouble.

Before she could form the words, Lush Fillpot, who must have been thinking the exact same thing, said, "We'd better ride."

# 20

"Just sit still, damn it," Fargo growled again.

Weasel sat down again and grimaced. "I can do somethin', can't I? Don't like feelin' so gull-durn helpless!"

"Just sit there," Fargo said through clenched teeth. "Trust me, that'll help."

He'd managed to make quite a bit of headway. The space between the old rockfall and the area in which they were trapped was about twelve feet, from end to end. He'd been able to pile the stones he pulled from the wall atop the rubble along one side of the tunnel. Working doggedly, he'd made his way back about another four feet. That was, up until Weasel had roused and decided to help.

He took another swig from the canteen and mopped at his brow. "I think I'm almost through to them," he said in a more kindly tone. He settled the cap on the canteen with the flat of his hand.

"Air's gone sour," remarked Weasel.

"It's from the cave," Fargo said. "That's how I know somebody's alive in there. Aside from the singing."

Weasel's face screwed up. "Singin'? I thought *I* was hearin' things."

"It was there." Fargo was tired, so tired. It seemed there was no muscle in his body that didn't scream with each and every move he made. He figured he'd have to get better to die.

" 'Spose you're thinkin' this is all my fault," Weasel said.

Fargo shook his head. "No, Weasel."

"Well, what was I supposed to think, when them yahoos come at me, wavin' a pair'a long underwear on a stick? You're the one what left me up there with no gun, y'know!"

"I know, Weasel," he said. His eyes were fluttering closed and he had to open them by sheer force of will. "You've already told me."

A flag of truce; that's what those long johns on the stick had been meant to signify, but Weasel had turned and run, and somebody got nervous. Shots had been fired, and now here they were, locked up in the bowels of the earth.

He just hoped that the men who'd rig up a white flag out of underwear would also try to dig them out. Or at least get out of the way for the rescue party that Clementine was bringing.

He wanted to sleep, to float off and dream of Clementine. Dream of her face, her hair, those round breasts and that creamy skin, wanted to dream of holding her again and . . .

Weasel poked him in the leg. Unfortunately, it was his sore one, and he yelped.

"Don't you go dozin' off on me, Fargo," the old trapper growled.

Fargo grunted.

"Well, *I* didn't go to sleep," Weasel went on indignantly, although Fargo hadn't said a word. "I was just passed out, that's all. A fella gets hisself shot, he's entitled to pass out."

Fargo stood up into his slouch and began to worm his way back into the rocks again. He was clearing just enough room for one man, lying on his belly, to pass through. No sense in clearing any more than that.

While Weasel continued to talk, he carefully freed another rock, and then wriggled backward with it. To the best of his calculations, he was almost there.

Back in the cave, Clay Reeves had long since stopped singing. Not because he wasn't feeling wildly musical, which he was, but because his throat had become so dry from his earlier efforts that he was pretty sure it was bleeding. He knew his lips were. He couldn't remember when they'd first cracked and split.

Tucker was with him, there in the dark. Good old Farley.

Good old ghost.

Why, Tucker'd even sung harmony with him on that last chantey. Good, strong bass voice, he had, even if he did foul up the words sometimes.

Into the darkness, he croaked, "You'll have to take the next one alone, Tucker. My voice is givin' out on me."

And Tucker replied, "Why, that's fine with me, Reeves, just fine. Rest yourself. Oh, and hold my knife for me while I sing, would you?"

Clay felt the little knife in his hand, ran his fingers over it. Funny, Tucker having a pocketknife exactly like his. But then, you never could tell about old Tucker. Who would have guessed that he knew every song Clay did?

"Might want'a flip out the blade," Tucker whispered. His voice seemed to come from everywhere, from the very rocks themselves. Probably a trick of the stone walls. "Might want to whet it a little. There on your wrist's fine."

He opened the blade and felt it with his thumb. It was even worn concave in the center, just like his.

"What you gonna sing, Farley?" Reeves asked.

"Thought maybe I'd do 'The Sea Widow's Lament,'" came the reply. "Why don't you get to stropping that blade, old son? There, roll up your cuff first. It's better on skin. That's my boy!"

Tucker's voice had changed, just slightly. It seemed to Reeves that there was a touch of his grandfather's burr creeping in. Funny.

He rested the blade against his wrist.

"No, the other side, laddie," crooned Tucker, sounding now exactly like his grandfather. He was in the walls, in the stone, everywhere. "Cut deep, make a clean job of it!"

"Grampa?" he whispered.

"Show me you're a man, bucko."

Reeves tried to swallow, but came up dry. "Where's Tucker?" he rasped. "Where'd he go?"

His grandfather's voice fairly roared in his ears, "Cut yourself, y'stupid bastard! D'you wish to fester away to naught down here in the Devil's own eternal blackness? Don't you hear Old Scratch diggin' for you right this very minute? He's comin' to snatch you down deep, laddie, snatch you straight down into the lake of fire and damnation, and yank you under. Don't you deserve it, boy? Haven't you killed enough innocents to qualify? He's nearly here, don't you have ears? Cut, laddie!" he said, his tone growing suddenly ominous. "Cut yourself quick or I'll take me strap to your backside!"

Reeves poised the blade. Grampa knew best.

But just as it bit into his flesh, a thin beam of light flashed over his face. It startled him, and he dropped the knife. It clattered on the stone floor and he groped for it wildly. Satan himself was coming in a beam of light, conjured from the fires of hell.

His fingers touched the blade, but he was too anxious and it skittered away. He fell back to see dust motes floating in the brightening beam of light. No, not dust motes. Stars, millions of stars, cast into the blinding brightness of eternal damnation.

"Can anybody hear me?" said a voice from outside, from beyond.

"Get away, get away!" Reeves tried to shout, but no sound emerged. He scarcely noticed. He was too busy crawling, falling, feeling his way, and scrambling weakly around that gigantic pile of silver ore, desperately trying to hide from the Beast of Darkness bathed in light at the wall.

Despite Lush's shouted warnings that she stop, Clementine broke away from the others and fanned the Ovaro into her father's old camp.

Leaping from the horse's back, she ran to a man coming out of the tunnel and began to pound on him with her fists.

"Who are you? What are you doing? Where's that son of a bitch Daggett!"

The fellow was so startled that he dropped the stone he was lugging on his foot. He yelped and began to hop on one leg, ignoring her entirely.

At just about the time she began to realize that nobody had so much as leveled a gun on her, a voice called out, "Miss? Miss, over here!"

She looked toward the spring. A tall, clean-shaven man was coming toward her.

"Who's in charge here?" she demanded, striding toward him. "Who are these men, and where's—"

The man didn't seem to register her question, but instead grabbed her wrist, stopping her in midsentence, and dragged her toward the trees.

"Hey!" she shouted. "Stop that! Just who do you think you are?"

But she stopped shouting when she saw the old man on the ground, in the shade of the paloverdes. He was sick, maybe dying, and a young man sat beside him with his hat in his hands, weeping silently.

"You can witness this," the tall man said, and thrust

a Bible and a thick, stubby pencil at her. She took them dumbly, and he said, "On the fly leaf. In back."

She opened it.

"I, Zebulon Jackson Daggett, being of sound mind but about ready to shed this mortal coil, do hereby dictate my last will and testament . . ."

She read it, then looked up. "Who's Luke Shepherd?"

The tall man colored and said, "I guess I am."

Behind her, she heard the sounds of slowing hooves as the others rode into the camp, but she paid them no mind. She just kept looking at Luke Shepherd, and she felt nothing but disgust. She said, "Convenient, isn't it?"

"Ma'am?"

"Him leaving you everything. He's the richest man in the territory! How do I know that—"

The old man looked up at her, his eyes slitted, and motioned for her to come closer. She bent to him.

Leaning down, her ear to his lips, she heard him whisper, "What's your name, girl?"

"Clementine," she said crisply. "Clementine Mc-Bride." This was the man who had ordered her father's death. She'd listen to him, but she didn't have to like it.

"Pretty," he said.

She waited, lips tight.

"Witness it, please," he went on, each word an effort. "I may be old and I may be dying, but I have got my right mind about me." He closed his eyes again. "Just sign," he whispered.

She sat up, craning her head back toward Shepherd. "I'll sign it," she snapped, "but it's wrong. You've got to strike out one sentence first."

Shepherd sighed. "Never mind. I'll get one'a the boys. Paco!" he shouted. "Stop jumpin' around on one foot and get down here!"

"Strike that sentence!" she insisted.

"Who the hell are you, anyway, lady?" Just then,

he seemed to take note of all the hubbub up at the entrance to the shaft, and of the men that were not his own. "And where in tarnation did all these men come from?"

"They came to help dig," she said. "Now, strike that sentence. It's the one that begins, 'This is to include the—'"

Paco, favoring one foot, came skidding down to the spring. "What you want, Shepherd?" He glanced down at Daggett, and removed his hat. He leaned in, and in a softer tone, he asked, "Is he . . . ?"

"Not yet," replied Shepherd. He wrenched the Bible and lead from Clementine, and thrust them at Paco. "Back flyleaf. Need you to witness his will."

"No!" Clementine shouted. "Not until you strike that—"

"Shut up!" Shepherd shouted.

Paco handed the Bible, unopened, back to Shepherd. He shrugged. "Can't read," he said.

Clementine crossed her arms and smiled smugly.

Someone touched her shoulder and she wheeled. It was Lush Fillpot.

"There's a problem, miss," he said, and when she just stared at him, he said, "I've been speaking with the gentlemen up at the tunnel. I'm afraid there's been another cave-in. Weasel and Fargo are trapped in there."

It felt as if a cold hand had suddenly taken hold of all her internal organs and wrenched them from her body. She staggered and Lush caught her. He sat her down across from Daggett.

"Sign this," she heard Shepherd say, as if from a great distance, and a shadow passed overhead as he handed the Bible to Lush.

She didn't try to stop him from witnessing the will. It didn't matter now, nothing mattered, not the paper in her pocket, none of it.

Lush bent down to her. "Miss Clementine?" he said

gently. "There are a whole lot of men up there, and they're making good time. We'll get to them quickly, you just wait and see."

She nodded, then touched his arm. He had to be worried, too. After all, Weasel was in there along with Fargo. She didn't say what she knew he was thinking: that if the previous cave-ins were any example, they'd more than likely find Fargo's and Weasel's bodies.

Crushed beyond recognition.

The boy who'd been sitting with Daggett cleared his throat and said, in a broken voice, "Mr. Shepherd? He's gone, sir."

Shepherd knelt slowly. He whispered something she couldn't hear to the body, then eased the thin blanket up, covering the face. He held his hat low on his chest for a moment. Then, to the boy, he said, "All right, Jim. Best get to digging."

He stood then, settling his hat on his head, and he was as weary and wrung out with grief as she'd ever seen a man. For just a second she felt sorry for him.

It was just a second, though.

And then something seemed to go *click* behind Shepherd's eyes. He looked down at her, and at Lush. "Did you say *Fargo* was trapped in that shaft?"

Lush nodded. "Him and my partner, Weasel Smith."

"*Skye* Fargo?"

Eyes narrowed, Clementine looked up and nodded. He had her attention.

Shepherd grabbed his hat off his head and slapped his leg with it, and both Clementine and Lush jumped.

"Of all the stupid, low-down, ornery, pig-headed, thieving sons of bitches!" he shouted.

Lush said, "You know him?"

Clementine was about to argue the point when Shepherd added, "Know him? That furry-faced jackass saved my hide along the Colorado River, that's all! Rode with him for two months until he got side-tracked by some fancy Spanish skirt over in California.

Yeah, I should say I know him. But what the hell possessed him to try and steal this silver mine?"

"I've been trying to tell you, you idiot!" shouted Clementine. She yanked the paper from her pocket and threw it at him. It fluttered at his feet. "It's *my* silver mine," she said, "and I've got the filing papers to prove it! Daggett's land stops five whole miles north of here."

"So that's what you were doing in town!" she heard Lush whisper, but she was too busy, too angry, and too upset to acknowledge it.

"Fargo wasn't stealing anybody's silver," she went on, all in a rush. "It was my daddy's and my uncle's, except that Sheriff Tucker and his deputy murdered them on *his* orders." She pointed at the blanketed form. "And then the Apaches came and I thought they were going to skin us but then didn't, and the mine caved in and we tried to dig out Tucker and Reeves except that it caved in again and I had to go get help, and . . . and . . ."

She couldn't go on, for the tears had started flowing down her cheeks in earnest, and her throat closed up.

Lush's arm circled around her and she leaned into him, sobbing.

Above her, she heard Shepherd mutter, "Damn," and then he walked off, toward the mine. "Let's move it, boys," she heard him shout. "Double time! We've got a whole new set of victims inside, and they've been down there for a whole lot longer than I want to think about."

## 21

Fargo moved the final rock and wormed his way into the cave, his skinned back and bruised hip and leg crying out at every small movement. It was dark as pitch despite the thin light coming from the crawl-hole behind him, and as soon as he'd scrambled down the rocks and debris to the floor of the cave, he called, "Weasel? Can you hand me the lamp?"

He'd tunneled through at the top of the shaft, for its ceiling—at this point, anyway—was pretty much solid rock. He didn't relish the thought of another rock slide.

He waited while Weasel, sounding farther away than he was, grumbled and groused about his shoulder, about the lamp, about the narrowness of the crawl space. And while he waited, he tried to see through the gloom. He could pick out, just faintly, the outline of the ore pile, which was bigger than he remembered. But that was all.

"Anybody here?" he asked the darkness. "Tucker? Reeves?"

If they weren't in the cave, then they were crushed beneath the last few feet of rock blocking the tunnel. But they couldn't be under the rock. At least, not both of them.

Somebody had been singing.

Ghosts?

An involuntary shudder swept through him, but

Fargo shook off the chill. That was crazy. He was just tired, that was all. He'd been down here too long.

"Tucker?" he said again. No answer. "Reeves?"

Weasel was inching toward him, and belatedly he realized he should have made the passage a little broader: Weasel's bony shoulders were as wide as the butt end of a draft mare. But the light was growing closer now, and he could see a little better.

The ore pile gradually altered from an faint outline into a solid mass. But still, there was no one to be seen.

"Here, dang it!" said Weasel. The lantern, dangling from a hand, came through the hole he'd just crawled out of, and suddenly, he could see the whole chamber.

And Tucker's body, lying twisted on the buckled stone of the floor.

"Found one of 'em," he said softly, and took the lantern from Weasel's outstretched hand.

"That's fine and dandy, but I ain't going no further down this death trap a'yourn than I got to," Weasel's voice grouched as he backed away, down the crawl space. "I'd druther be in the dark than get squeezed to death."

Fargo paid him scant attention. Holding the lantern, he knelt beside Tucker, and then frowned.

This man sure as hell hadn't been doing any singing. He'd been dead a long time, maybe since the first cave-in. His leg was twisted at an unnatural angle— likely broken at the time of the slide, Fargo thought. And there were livid marks at his throat.

Rocks hadn't done that.

There was a small scuffling sound from behind the mound of ore. Fargo stiffened.

"Reeves?" he said.

The sound came again, and Fargo turned just in time to see Reeves launching himself through the air.

He hit Fargo before he was completely up out of his crouch, and the two men went tumbling over Tucker's body. The lantern flew, too, and smashed against the wall. Flames raced along the floor, following the path of spilled kerosene.

Reeves's hands were at his throat, but Fargo twisted away, wrenching himself free. He rolled on his back, through the kerosene fire. Though the raw skin complained loud and sharp, he kept rolling until he was out of Reeves's reach.

But he could see that Reeves was wild-eyed, crazy. He'd gone mad in the darkness, and possessed the strength of the insane. Awkwardly, Reeves got to his feet, and then he walked through the dwindling flames toward Fargo, murder in his narrowed, bloodshot eyes.

Fargo edged around the mound of ore. He could hear Weasel shouting "Fargo? Fargo!" but he didn't answer. He'd just realized that Reeves was holding a very familiar Arkansas toothpick.

Without thinking, he dropped to a crouch and felt his boot sheath. Empty.

*God damn it!*

He didn't have long to think, though, because Reeves opened his mouth, emitting a dry, croaking sound that Fargo supposed was meant to be a war cry of sorts. And then he charged.

Fargo jumped aside at the last moment, taking the brunt of the charge in his right shoulder, and spun Reeves around. He felt the blade skitter along his arm, and shoved it away just as the last of the firelight died.

Now they were in the dark, struggling on the cold stone floor. First Fargo had the upper hand, then Reeves, then Fargo again.

Hands locked on the knife, they rolled hard against the ore pile, and rocks bit into Fargo's already injured back. Wincing with pain, he threw his bad leg over Reeves's hip, locked it, and twisted with all his might.

The move took Reeves by surprise, and for a split second Fargo felt Reeves's grip on the blade falter.

He took full advantage of it, twisting the knife to the side, pulling it free of Reeves's grasping fingers.

And then Reeves was gone. Like a vapor, he evaporated into the pitch black of eternal underground night.

Fargo held his breath, listening. He'd lost his bearings during the scuffle. Reeves might be anywhere.

Slowly, silently, he got to his feet. He held the toothpick close to his waist, the blade ready.

And then he heard a dry rasp of air, the sound of a near-silent cry of rage, and the thud of boot steps as Reeves charged again. He ducked to what he hoped was one side, but this time Reeves was ready for him. Reeves bulled into him, knocking him off his feet and back into a wall, and they both went sprawling.

And then they lay still. Grunting with the effort and ignoring the agony in his back as best he could, he shoved Reeves off him. Reeves rolled to the side, and as he toppled away, he felt his knife, now buried to the hilt between Reeves's ribs.

The son of a bitch had run right into it.

Still panting, he tugged his blade free. He heard the soft, sucking sound the insulted flesh made in the darkness, and cleaned the knife off on Reeves's pants leg. He slid it home, into its boot sheath.

And then he leaned forward, hands on his legs and head down.

Some rescue party! They'd found their man alive, only to kill him—and with him, Fargo's only alibi for the double murder of the McBrides.

"Fargo?" Weasel's voice was distant, and small with apprehension.

"What?" he said wearily.

"You alive?"

"For the time being."

There was silence for a moment, then Weasel said, "Not to make you think I'm pryin' or anything, but you wanna tell me what all that tusslin' was about?"

Fargo had never in his life felt so weary, or so torn apart. Every inch of his hide smarted and there was fire in every muscle. He crawled forward, then stretched out on his stomach on the cool stone. "Later, Weasel."

"Later! What you mean, later? I'm up here all by my lonesome, don't know who's dead or killed, and all you can say is later!"

"Later, Weasel," he muttered again, and then he was asleep.

The sun had nearly set, but the work hadn't stopped. Men formed a living chain down the tunnel, passing rocks hand to hand, hauling out loads of sand and gravel and dirt and pebbles.

Clementine sat beside the fire, stirring the stew pot and brewing coffee. She was running on nothing but sheer nerve, now. She had busied herself with cooking, and the men were eating in shifts. Currently, Luke Shepherd and Lush Fillpot were beside her, bolting down plates of cornbread and rabbit stew.

She glanced up and saw the boy, Jim, walking down to the fire, and started to get a plate ready before she realized that he'd eaten only a half hour earlier. She stuck the spoon back in the stew pot and looked up at him expectantly, as she'd looked at every man that came out of the mine.

"Mr. Shepherd?" he said, after he nodded to her. "We're through to 'em."

Her heart in her throat, Clementine listened while Shepherd asked the all-important question. "Are they all right?"

Jim's face screwed up. "Two dead. Two kinda banged up, but Harley says—"

"They'll live," came Harley's voice, just as he stepped from the mine's entrance. Another man was with him, and they held up Weasel Smith between them. Filthy, his hair caked with dust, he was naked

145

from the waist up, and when he saw Clementine, he said indignantly, "What you polecats doin', bringin' me out here half-nekkid when there's a female about?"

Tears of relief pushing at his eyes, Lush went to his side straight away.

"Be careful, gull-durn it!" Weasel roared. "Can't you see that I'm shot?"

They brought him over to the fire and wrapped him in a blanket after Lush took a peek at his shoulder and pronounced the wound minor.

"I'll dig that out for you," Lush offered.

"Not till after I've et," said Weasel, eyeing the stew. "And who in tarnation stole your chin whiskers? They got your hair, too!"

There was still no sign of Fargo, and Clementine was afraid to ask Weasel, afraid of what he might tell her. Slowly, she rose and walked toward the tunnel. Her feet felt for all the world like lead, and her joints seemed to have turned to clammy mush.

And then, just when she'd finally made it to the mouth of the mine and was just stepping inside, they came into sight—Fargo, borne up by a man on either side.

A whimper of relief escaping her lips, she ran toward him on limbs she'd thought could go no farther. She threw her arms around him, weeping hysterically.

He winced, but winked at her. "Hello, darlin'," he said. "Miss me?"

All she could do was weep, "Fargo, oh Fargo!"

"Be careful, ma'am," warned one of the men holding him up. It was Mike from town, the man with the handlebar mustache. Gently, he pushed her away. "He's got a back scraped up like I ain't never seen," he said as they started forward again. "Took the hide clean off it. Think maybe his leg's broke, too."

"Bring him to the cookfire," she said, hurrying

ahead to lay out blankets. When the men caught up to her, she'd already made a place.

"Easy, easy!" she cautioned as they set him down.

"Do I smell rabbit stew?" Fargo asked weakly. Then, "Well, I'll be a son of a bitch! Luke Shepherd?"

"You can do your catching up later," Clementine said. She motioned at Shepherd to fix him a plate, then she took a lantern and moved behind him to inspect the damage.

What she saw made her ache for him. The flesh between his shoulder blades—and a strip as wide as her hand and extending nearly to his waist—was completely denuded of skin. Its raw and dirty flesh was embedded with bloody pebbles and grit, and it was already beginning to seep fluid that wept crimson trails through the grime.

"Water," she called out to anyone close enough to hear. She was already busy going through her pack, looking for her tweezers and a jar of unguent. "Water, lots of it, and rags. How's your leg, Fargo?"

"Been better," he said around a mouthful of stew.

"I mean, is it broken?" She found the unguent.

"Don't think so," he said. "Weasel, you want to pour me some of that coffee?"

"How can you think about coffee at a time like—"

"Deputy Simpson?" Fargo broke in. "You gonna arrest me?"

Simpson shook his head. "Miss Clementine and Pa explained. I'm right sorry for bustin' your door in the other day, but—"

"Pa?" Fargo asked. "Who's your pa?"

"I'll explain later," said Clementine as Shepherd set a pan of water and a few rags beside her. She dipped one in and gave it a good wringing. "It's a long story, Fargo, and you'll want to be all the way awake to hear it. Trust me."

And then, to the tune of Fargo's sudden stream of curses, she began to clean his back.

## 22

When Fargo woke, it was in a bed under a soft quilt, and he saw he was in a house. Through the window he saw a sunlit clearing. Beyond, the towering ponderosa pines were busy with birds. Daggett's place, he guessed. No, Luke Shepherd's, now. He seemed to remember Clementine explaining it.

As he sat up, more memories flooded back, little snips of things—the trip up the mountain on a travois, somebody feeding him broth, Clementine changing his bandages and telling him not to be such a baby.

He smiled.

He pulled himself over to sit on the edge of the bed. His back still hurt, but it was a good bit better than it had been before. The soreness had gone out of his muscles, too, and all that was left was a lingering stiffness. Well, a little exercise would take care of that.

He stood up, then fell back again. Dizzy as a newborn colt, and somebody'd swiped his britches, too!

"Hey!" he yelled at the closed door. "Hey, somebody!" and remembered to cover himself when the door started to open.

It was Clementine, but like he'd never seen her. She was wearing a pink dress that clung to her bodice like she'd been poured into it. Plump breasts threatened to spill from a neckline that would have been modest on anybody but her, and her glossy, nearly black hair was piled high on her head in thick ringlets.

He must have been staring with a wolfish gleam in his eye, because she flushed the same pink as her frock and said, "Welcome back to the land of the living, Fargo."

He couldn't do anything but look at her, and she went on. "We're at the Inca Land and Cattle Company's headquarters. Mr. Shepherd is very kindly letting us stay on until you're healed up. Now, let me take a look at that back."

She did, and from behind him, she said, "You must have been born under a lucky star, Fargo. There was a good bit more skin left than I thought at first. You're practically healed!"

He was suddenly feeling a good bit better, and said, "If you want to reach around front, Clem, there's some skin there that needs tending, too."

She put her hands on his shoulders, and he felt her breath on his ear as she said, "Naughty, naughty. There'll be time for that later on." She leaned away, and he felt the bed creak before she stepped into view again. "Get dressed, Fargo. You've been lying in this feather bed for four days. It's about time you took some fresh air into your lungs!"

He blinked. *"Four days?"* It seemed impossible.

She nodded. "Your clothes are in the chifforobe. We cleaned them, and cleaned you up, too. I'll be waiting on the front porch. And while we walk, I'll tell you everything I know, I promise." She smiled, and it lit up the whole room.

"Clementine?" he said as she turned to go out the door.

"Yes, Fargo?"

"You look like a million dollars."

She blushed again. "And that's just about what I'm worth, give or take."

"What?"

"Get dressed, Fargo."

Then she was gone.

*   *   *

They walked down through the pines, and Fargo felt more himself with every step. As Clementine gathered wildflowers for the table, she explained about Lush's reunion with his son, Josh, and what she'd had to do in the bar to get anybody to listen to her.

Fargo grinned when he heard this. "Now, just how'd you do that?" he teased, reaching for her. "You just opened your shirt wide, you say?"

Laughing, she moved away, her hands shielding her breasts. "All things in good time, Fargo. Don't you go fouling up my plans, now!"

She told him about her trip to file the claim, and how she'd been right—Daggett's land had stopped five miles north of the Santa Rosa. She'd found the mine and the surrounding land was free for the taking. It was hers, now, legally. Nobody could dispute it.

"And you just rode off and left it to come up here?" he asked, incredulously. "Every yahoo north of the Mexican border'll be riding up to steal a piece of it!"

She shook her head. "Mr. Shepherd took care of that. He's posted a guard, and after you're better—and I'm not so distracted—he's going help me to put together a wagon train to haul what's already dug to the smelter at Chino, and to hire miners to dig the rest of the ore out. He says there'll be some trouble with the cathedral room—the walls in there are amazing, Fargo! I never got to see them before. Did you?"

He shook his head.

"Well," she continued enthusiastically, "they're practically solid silver ore! I can't believe Daddy and Uncle Tyrone never looked!" Her brow furrowed slightly, and she added, "Mr. Shepherd said it wasn't like Mr. Daggett to send anybody to kill Daddy and Uncle Tyrone. It wasn't something he'd do. I'm inclined to believe him. Mr. Shepherd says that Daggett had been sick for a long time, and maybe he wasn't himself when he talked to Sheriff Tucker. Maybe he used a poor choice of words, and Sheriff Tucker just assumed . . ."

She paused, and Fargo saw that she was struggling to hold back her tears. A change of subject was in order. "So I've got the Jupiter constabulary off my back for good?"

"Yes," she said. "Deputy Simpson checked with the postmistress, and there was no letter waiting to go out. She said she hadn't even seen the sheriff all week."

Fargo snorted. It figured. All this, and for nothing.

"How's your leg?" Clementine asked. She was standing in a shaft of light that beamed down through the branches, and she practically glowed.

*Well*, he thought, *it wasn't* exactly *for nothing*.

He gave a kick to a nearby pine. "Right as rain. My back feels pretty damn good, too."

"Good," she said, moving toward him. "We'd better get back. You're going to like Mrs. Vasquez's cooking." She reached him, and stood on her tiptoes to kiss him, but when he tried to deepen it, she pulled away and giggled like a schoolgirl. "Not yet, Fargo," she teased, and ran ahead of him, up toward the house.

*Women*, he thought, then shook his head. Grinning, he followed after her.

Lush Fillpot and Weasel Smith weren't in attendance, having gone with Lush's son to Jupiter, but Fargo and Clementine and Shepherd enjoyed a fine meal. Afterward, accompanied by a couple of the best cigars he'd seen in a long while and a bottle of imported brandy, he and Shepherd continued their reminiscing out on the porch for a good two hours.

At last, Fargo stood up and stretched. Darkness had fallen over the mountains a good while back, and the cool night air was still and quiet. Only the occasional hoot of an owl or the faraway howl of a coyote broke the silence.

Shepherd stood up along with him. "You leaving in the morning?" he asked.

Fargo grinned. "Does it show?"

"You never were one for sticking around. Always on the move."

Fargo shrugged. "My feet get itchy."

Shepherd leaned against the porch rail. "Seems to me that gal in there could scratch 'em for you. Not that it's any of my business."

"I've been tempted," Fargo admitted. "Believe me. Still, when it comes right down to it . . ."

Shepherd nodded. "Well, your stud's in fine fettle. We've been letting him graze in the paddock every day, and Jim curried him up to a spit shine just this afternoon. He's down at the barn anytime you want to pick him up."

"Thanks, Luke," Fargo said, and opened the door. He paused halfway through it, though. He turned back toward Shepherd and said softly, "You'll watch after her for a spell?"

Shepherd nodded solemnly. "Maybe more."

Fargo walked back through the quiet house, down the long dark hall to the room he'd been given to use. He was a little surprised when he didn't find Clementine there, waiting for him. But nonetheless, he groped his way to the bed, found the nightstand and the matches, and lit his lamp.

"About time you stopped jawing and came to bed," purred Clementine's sultry voice. She'd been under the covers the whole time.

He sat beside her and touched her face, brushing the dark hair back. He smiled. "Glad you waited for me, darlin'."

"I wanted you to make love to me in a real bed," she said softly, and she was smiling, just a little around the corners of her mouth. "The wide open spaces have their place, Fargo, but nothing beats a feather mattress for sheer comfort."

"Is that right?" he asked, and let his hand trail down to her chest and the top of the quilt. Slowly, he pulled it down to her waist. She was completely nude.

Gently, his hands traced the contours of her body, lingered at the full breasts, toyed briefly with their nipples, glanced over her ribs and stomach, then slowly pulled the quilt the rest of the way down, leaving her completely naked.

He lay one hand on the dark delta between her legs, and remembered what he'd thought the first time he'd seen her without her clothes—that she was a woman a man would want to keep naked twenty-four hours a day. Now, seeing her lie languorous and unashamed against clean, white sheets, her dark hair fanning across the pillows and those ripe, beaded breasts washed by lamplight, he knew he'd been right all along.

"You're beautiful, Clem," he whispered, in what he knew was a vast understatement.

"I'm cold, Fargo," she said with just a trace of a come-hither smile. "Why don't you cover me with something? Yourself, for instance."

"Yes, ma'am," he said, and bent to kiss her.

He shucked out of his buckskins and joined her on the mattress and the cool, clean sheets, and then he kissed her again, long and hard. He found he couldn't wait, and after suckling her breast for a few seconds, he turned her onto her stomach.

"Fargo?" she said. "What are you—"

"Shhh," he whispered, and hopped down, off the bed. He pulled her partway off its high edge, until her feet were on the floor and her bottom was at the level of his hips, and then he took her from behind, sliding into her easily.

She gasped with the surprise of it, and then she tilted her pelvis and began to shove backward, raising her hips, matching him thrust for thrust. He felt her start to pull and tug at him, to ripple over his member as he rode her. He clutched at those glorious buttocks, and kept riding her.

"Yes, Fargo," she whispered hoarsely. "Yes!"

And then he exploded with an almost blinding suddenness, and his last two thrusts nearly lifted her off the bed. Vaguely, he was aware that she shuddered too, and when he opened his eyes and helped her roll over, he saw that she was slit-eyed and smiling.

"You're a constant surprise," she purred, panting a little. "Where did you have in mind for next time? The pump stand?"

He chuckled and gave her leg a little swat, and giggling, she pulled herself up and over to the far pillow.

He lay down beside her. "Next time, we'll *both* be on the bed."

"Promise?" she asked. She propped herself on one arm and leaned over to kiss his chest.

"I promise."

She was kissing his belly now, flicking his navel with her tongue. "Good boy," she said, and crept lower.

He knew where she was headed, and it wasn't long before she was there, taking his shaft into her hot, wet mouth, then pulling it out, licking its length and ringing the head with her tongue.

"Clem?" he said, even as he felt himself stir to life again.

It was her turn to hush him, and he obeyed, waiting quietly until the sensation of her heated tongue, her gently raking teeth, and the suction of her lips was nearly more than he could bear. Just when he could no longer stand it, she stopped. It took every ounce of self-control he owned to keep from pushing her head back to business.

But he staved off the impulse, and after she kissed and nipped and licked her way up his torso, he gathered her into his arms. "Clem?" he whispered. "You're something else."

She bit his ear, worrying it with her teeth. He answered by rolling her onto her back and nipping lightly at her pink and swollen nipples, then nuzzling the undersides of her breasts, feeling their soft weight against his face.

And then he was on top of her, between her open legs, entering her for the second time. They rocked together on that feather bed, rising, rising; rising until they both could rise no further and the whole world, for one instant, stopped still for them.

In the morning, well before the sun had risen, Fargo was up and dressed. Shepherd had said the Ovaro was rested and ready. Before long, he and the stallion would be on the trail, headed south for the border country.

His bedroll under one arm and his saddlebags across one shoulder, he paused to look at Clementine in the dim lamplight. He should have said good-bye, but he couldn't bring himself to do it. Let her sleep, he told himself. Shepherd could tell her when she woke. Shepherd could comfort her.

After all, the man had his plans.

Well, Shepherd was the put-down-roots sort.

Clementine opened her eyes, and he found he couldn't move.

Her eyes flicked down to the saddlebags, then back up to his face. "So soon?" was all she said.

"Yeah."

"I'll miss you, Fargo." No hysterics, no drama. Just the statement, pure and simple. She understood, then.

"I'll miss you, too, Clementine," he said, and he meant it more than he realized.

"Take care of yourself, Fargo," she whispered. "And for God's sake, the next time somebody asks you to mail a letter for them, think twice about it, all right?"

He chuckled, the sound welling up in his throat so quickly that he couldn't stifle it. "I won't have to think twice," he said. "Not if there's a chance it'll lead me to somebody like you."

Before she had a chance to answer him, he stepped through the door and closed it behind him. The house was dark, but he found the front door and let himself out.

Once he'd reached the barn and saddled the Ovaro and set out on the long ride to the south, the newborn sun was sending fingers of light through the pines, and he was still thinking about that dark-haired beauty he'd left behind.

He shook his head. "They call you the Trailsman, Fargo," he muttered in disgust, "not the *Homes*man."

With a sudden whoop, he sank his heels into the Ovaro and cantered south, into the wide, vast unknown.

**LOOKING FORWARD!**
**The following is the opening**
**section from the next novel in the exciting**
*Trailsman* **series from Signet:**

**THE TRAILSMAN #220**

**MONTANA GUN SHARPS**

*Montana, 1860, where desperate men ply their trade*
*with quick triggers, and the word of one man*
*stands as law on a lawless frontier. . . .*

The big man in buckskins reined up beside a crude
wooden sign. His piercing lake-blue eyes rose to the fork
just ahead and the rutted excuse for a road that wound
to the north, then he glanced down again at the sign.
"Silver Flats," he read aloud to his Ovaro. "Two miles."
Skye Fargo had never heard of the place, which wasn't
unusual. Based on its name, he guessed it must be a
boom town, and boom towns were like weeds these days.
They sprang up wherever a strike was claimed, saw their
day in the sun, and withered as soon as the ore played
out. Ordinarily he would have passed Silver Flats by
without a second thought, but he had been on the trail
for weeks and his stallion could use a day or two of rest.
So, for that matter, could he.

In no great hurry, Fargo reined northward, holding to a walk. The morning sun was warm on his back and the lush forest on either side was alive with the chirping of birds and the occasional chittering of squirrels. All seemed peaceful, yet Fargo never let down his guard. He had no hankering to go to an early grave, and staying alert was the key to staying alive—in the wilds or close to civilization.

Before long, Fargo detected the acrid odor of smoke. His hand strayed to the butt of the Colt on his hip as he straightened in the saddle. After another hundred yards, he heard voices. Coming around a bend, he saw three men hunkered around a fire in a crescent-shaped clearing on the left. Fargo's wariness flared, tightening his gut. The three had the unmistakable stamp of hardcases. It showed in their flinty faces, in their low-slung revolvers, and in their coiled postures. They spotted him right away and all three rose, their hands hanging near their hardware.

Fargo intended to ride on by. Who they were and what they were up to was of no concern to him. All he was interested in was a cozy bed in a warm hotel room. After he treated himself to a few whiskeys, of course, and maybe an evening of cards. Not to mention the willing company of a fallen dove. But as he neared the clearing, the three curly wolves edged to the side of the road.

The shortest, a runt with a shock of red hair and cheeks dotted with large freckles, swaggered into the road, barring the pinto's way. He wore a big Remington and carried himself like a grown man, but Fargo guessed he couldn't be more than sixteen or seventeen years old, if that. Pushing his narrow-brimmed hat back on his head, he grinned good-naturedly. His tone held a different edge entirely. "Hold up there, stranger. We'd like a few words with you. Where might you be headed?"

Fargo drew rein. He supposed he could be civil, but

the pup's arrogance was grating. "None of your damn business."

The kid was smarter than he appeared. He didn't get mad or toss an insult back. Instead, his grin widened. "There's no call to get uppity, mister. I'm Billy Pardee. Maybe you've heard of me?"

"Can't say that I have." Fargo watched the other two closely. One was tall and lanky with eyes as cold as ice. The other was average in every respect except for a jagged scar down his left cheek. Neither showed any interest in unlimbering their irons, but Fargo wasn't taking anything for granted.

"Well, down in the Staked Plain country folks sure know me." Pardee said, sounding disappointed. "I've blown out the wicks of more hombres than I can count."

Fargo's opinion of the upstart fell even more. Only a jackass would brag about killing. "You're a long way from Texas."

Pardee chuckled. "It got a little too warm for comfort, if you savvy my meanin'. So my friends and me lit a shuck. Been ridin' the high lines ever since, blowin' wherever the winds takes us."

In other words, Fargo translated, the law was after them, probably because of the runt's itchy trigger finger.

"You have the look of a man who knows a teat from a tit," Pardee went on. "I reckon you must know these parts pretty well. We'd be obliged if you'd tell us how we can find Luther Teller."

"Don't know the man," Fargo said, lifting the reins. "I'm as new to this neck of the woods as you are." He'd made it plain he wanted to ride on but the runt didn't move from in front of the Ovaro.

"We heard tell he's lookin' for gents who are handy in a shootin' scrape," the young gunman mentioned.

"And you figure to hire on," Fargo guessed.

"Why not? It's what I do best, so why not get paid

for blowing windows in a few skulls? A man has to make a livin', doesn't he?"

"Ask me again when you *are* a man," Fargo rejoined. He didn't know what made him say it. He wasn't looking for trouble. But he had an overwhelming urge to put this runt in his place.

Billy Pardee stiffened, his grin fading. "Mister, you shouldn't go around insultin' people. Not unless you're partial to a lead diet."

"Should I tremble in fear now or later?"

The young gun shark glared, his arm hooked to claw at his six-shooter. "I don't eat crow for anyone, ever. You'll apologize . . . or else."

It was then that the man with the scar came to life. Stepping quickly to Pardee's side, he placed a restraining hand on his wrist. "We don't want no trouble, Billy, remember? We don't want to draw any attention to ourselves."

Pardee wrenched the man's hand off his arm. "Who's to know, Decker?"

"Keller might hear of it and we'll be out of a job," Decker said. "Remember, the word was to drift quietlike."

"He's right," said the tall drink of water with icy eyes.

Pardee continued to scowl at Fargo, his hand quivering above his revolver. Fargo was certain the Texan would slap leather, but again Pardee surprised him by lowering his arm and shrugging.

"Looks like I'm outvoted, stranger. We'll meet again, though. I'll make a point of it. And next time I won't sheathe my claws."

Fargo nudged the stallion with his knees. It moved forward so quickly that the freckle-faced gunman had to bound out of the way or be bowled over. Swiveling in the saddle, Fargo didn't take his eyes off the three gunmen until another bend hid them. Even then, he continued to check over his shoulder. Pardee didn't strike him as the sort who cared overly much whether he shot someone in the front or in the back. Only after a mile without incident did Fargo feel safe.

The forest ended at a broad strip of grassy flatland situated at the base of the Anaconda Range. The stark, rugged Rocky Mountains, covered with fir, pine and spruce, was a region scarcely explored let alone settled, home to grizzlies without number and hostiles without mercy. Several peaks glistened with caps of pristine snow.

But it was the town of Silver Flats at their base that interested Fargo most. It was bigger than he expected, with thirty to forty buildings, some no more than planks thrown together with high false fronts. As a boom town, it should have been bustling with activity but he only saw a handful of people abroad. Rather dull and drab, Fargo thought.

Fargo entered the wide main street, passing a stable, a general store, a butcher's, an inn named Etta's Lodgings, and a tack shop. Halting at a hitch rail in front of the town's saloon, he dismounted. A middle-aged woman was walking by and he touched the brim of his hat to her. She ignored him. Gazing up and down the street, he realized that all the other people out and about were women as well. There wasn't a man in sight.

Puzzled, Fargo removed his hat and used it to slap some of the dust from his buckskins. Then, licking his lips in anticipation, he ambled into the saloon and over to the bar. It was still early but Fargo expected to find at least a few thirsty souls present. Yet no one else was there. The saloon was empty save for a crusty old bartender who was polishing glasses with an air of total boredom.

"Where is everyone?" Fargo inquired.

The barkeep looked up. "Thunderation! I didn't hear you come in!" Beaming like a politician on the stump, he wiped his hands on his apron and beckoned. "Don't be shy, friend. Come on over. I haven't had a paying customer in so long, I'm about ready to start talking to myself."

His puzzlement growing, Fargo strolled to the counter. "How can that be in a town this size? Don't tell me the temperance movement has spread this far?"

"Hell, I wish that was all it was." The bartender thrust out a calloused hand. "Irish Mike is my handle. I've been pouring coffin varnish for more years than I care to recollect. Name your poison."

Fargo requested whiskey. A dog barked outside, the lone sound emphasizing how dead quiet the town was. By rights, Silver Flats should be filled with constant racket. "Has the silver played out? Most everyone pull up stakes and leave?" Fargo wondered aloud.

"Oh, not hardly, boyo," Irish Mike said, pouring three fingers' worth into a shot glass. "You're new to these parts or you'd know that most of the men are up at the mine. 'The Silverlode,' it's called."

"When do they get back? Sunset?"

"Lordy, I wish." Irish Mike treated himself to a glass. "No, they go up on Monday morning and don't return until Friday evening. That alone is bad enough. I have practically no customers all week and then more than I can handle over the weekend. But in the past two months it's gotten a lot worse. Men can't buy drinks with money they don't have."

Fargo raised the glass to his lips. Savoring a slow sip, he felt the welcome burning sensation spread down his throat into the pit of his stomach. "How's that again?"

"They haven't been paid. The owner is expecting money at any time. But between you and me, if it doesn't get here soon those miners are likely to walk off the job. Then this town will dry up and blow away with the wind."

The news was interesting but of no personal importance to Fargo. He polished off the first glass and gestured for another. In a way he was glad he had the place all to himself. He'd spend a quiet day or two to give the stallion time to rest up, then continue on to Butte.

"I came here thinking to make money hand over fist," Irish Mike was saying, "and for a while I did. So I reckon I shouldn't complain just because George Prescott has had a run of powerful bad luck."

"Who?"

"Prescott. The owner of the Silverlode Mine. Or, rather, the manager. He runs it for a powerful consortium from back East."

"Ever hear of a gent named Keller?" Fargo asked, remembering the name Billy Pardee had mentioned.

Irish Mike absently nodded. "Who hasn't? Luther Keller is Prescott's right-hand man. Second in charge at the mine. Got his start as—" The door squeaked and Irish Mike paused. "Well, speak of the devil. Here he comes now."

Fargo turned. Into the saloon stalked a broad-shouldered man in a gray suit and bowler. He had a thick bull neck and fleshy jowls like those of a bulldog. A pencil-thin mustache framed his slit of a mouth, and on his chin grew a neatly trimmed triangle of a beard. In his shadow stepped a swarthy man in dark range clothes who favored an ivory-handled Smith & Wesson.

"Mr. Keller!" Irish Mike declared. "This is a pleasant surprise. You haven't graced me with a visit in, oh, a week or better."

"Then I'm overdue, aren't I?" Keller came over but the other man hung back near the entrance, his thumbs hooked in his gunbelt.

"Do you hear me complaining?" Irish Mike joked. "Will it be your usual? Bourbon?"

"That will be fine." Keller was studying Fargo intently and trying not to be obvious, and was doing a poor job. "Hello," he said cordially. "I don't believe we've met."

"You're right," Fargo said, and poured himself another glass.

"Are you seeking work, by any chance?" Keller probed. "You don't strike me as a miner but we're always looking for good men at the Silverlode."

"No thanks." Fargo shifted. "But I did run into a gent from Texas earlier, camped east of here a ways. He wants to hire on with you. Said something about you needing men who are handy with guns." Curiosity more than anything else had prompted Fargo into fishing for information.

Luther Keller froze in the act of reaching for the bourbon. His jaw muscles twitching, he replied testily, "You must have been mistaken. What need would I have for short-trigger men? In case you haven't caught on yet, I'm in the mining business." He jerked a thumb at the dark man in the dark clothes. "Harvey there is the exception. We keep him on the payroll to deal with troublemakers."

"I heard that Texan plain as day," Fargo said. "He mentioned you by name. Strange that he didn't just ride on into town and ask around for you."

"And I say you're wrong." Keller was trying hard not to show his agitation. He downed his drink in a couple of gulps, then slapped some coins onto the bar. "I'll thank you not to go spreading that tale of yours around Silver Flats. A man in my position can't afford to have baseless rumors spread." Adjusting his bowler, he barreled on out with the swarthy gunman in tow.

"Now that was damned peculiar," Irish Mike remarked.

Fargo thought so, too, but he shrugged and carried the bottle to a table. "Any chance of getting a bite to eat?"

"I can have Flora make you something," Mike proposed. Cupping a hand to his mouth, he bellowed, "Flannigan! Get your adorable self out here! We've got us a paying customer!" He turned to Fargo, saying,

"She's a feisty gal. Lost her husband in a cave-in last year and needed the work to help support her brood. Don't take liberties and she won't bash in your skull with a frying pan."

Both of them chuckled as a big-boned but winsome woman, whose mane of raven hair tumbled to her shapely buttocks came through the door. She wore a homespun dress that clung to her more than ample bosom and swaying hips. A scrubbed-clean complexion and lively hazel eyes completed the image. "A real, live paying customer you say? And here I reckoned we'd seen the last of them this century."

"Pay her no mind," Irish Mike said. "Her tongue is as tart as her food."

"Mike O'Shay, I'm the best cook in the territory, and you darn well know it," Flora scolded, wagging a finger at him in reproach. She stopped at Fargo's table. He caught the scent of lilacs clinging to her clothes. "So. By the process of elimination you must be the customer in question."

"And hungry enough to eat a buffalo," Fargo quipped.

"Well, unless you plan to go kill your own, you'll have to settle for eggs and bacon, And there's fresh baked pie for dessert. How would that be, big man?"

Fargo liked her playful gaze and frank bearing. "Throw in a pot of coffee and you have a deal. Add a back rub and I'll pay double."

Flora arched an eyebrow. "Would you indeed? If I thought that was a proposition, I'd pick up that chair next to you and hit you with it. I'm a lady. The last lecherous male who forgot that little fact lost four front teeth."

"Even ladies like company now and then," Fargo bantered.

"Ah. What a marvel. A man who claims he knows how women think." Flora's hazel eyes twinkled. "You're one in a million. Most men believe women were put on earth to bedevil and confuse them."

"And most women think men were put here to test their patience," Fargo countered. He was rewarded with a rich, lusty laugh.

"I like you, big man," the beauty confessed. "So I'll tell you what. For being such a social rascal, you can have that slice of pie at no extra charge."

Irish Mike overheard her. "Hold on there, Flora. This is my establishment and I set the prices, not you."

"True," Flora said, heading for the back, "but I do the cooking and the baking. So if I want to show a customer a wee bit of kindness, you'll not be stopping me, Mike O'Shay."

The door swung shut and Irish Mike shook his head in amazement. "Boyo, she must really be partial to you. She's never given another customer so much as a wink and a nod in all the time I've known her."

Fargo hoped it was an omen of things to come. Rising, he made for the entrance. "I'll stable my horse and be right back." He figured once the stallion was bedded down, he could relax and see about doing the same. Pushing the door wide, he stepped to the hitch rail and started to unwrap the pinto's reins. A glimmer of bright light on the roof of the building across the dusty street caught Fargo's attention and he looked up. Poking over the edge was a rifle barrel—pointed squarely at him.

Instinctively, Fargo dived to one side just as the rifle boomed. The slug bit into the dirt behind him, missing him and the Ovaro by inches. Palming his Colt, he snapped off two swift shots that splintered wood just below the rifle barrel and caused the rifleman to retreat from view. Heaving upright, Fargo rushed across the street.

A sign on the front of the building identified it as the assayer's office. Fargo was about to burst in through the door when he heard a loud thump at the rear. Veering to the left, Fargo flew around it to the back just in time to glimpse a vague figure vanish between buildings further down. He gave chase, sprinting past a ladder that had been propped against the wall.

As Fargo's legs raced, so did his mind. Who was trying to kill him? And why? He had no enemies in Silver Flats that he knew of. Luther Keller was angry at him over the comments he'd made in the saloon, yet they hardly merited being shot at.

Reaching the gap into which the would-be killer had vanished, Fargo dug in his heels. It was well he did. Again the rifle blasted, the bullet buzzing by like an angry hornet. Fargo banged off a shot of his own and heard boots pound in flight.

Again Fargo hurtled in pursuit. He caught sight of a leg rounding a corner, but when he reached the same spot, no one was in sight. He ran from building to building, checking alleys and every possible place of concealment, but after ten minutes he had to concede that the rifleman had given him the slip.

Twirling the Colt into its holster, Fargo returned to the main street. A small crowd, consisting mostly of women, had gathered near the saloon. Among them were Irish Mike and Flora, as well as Luther Keller. But not Harvey, Keller's hired gun.

A heavyset fellow in a beige hat, faded vest, baggy shirt and loose-fitting pants, was telling everyone to stay calm, that there had to be a perfectly sound explanation for the shooting, and that he would get to the bottom of it. As Fargo approached, the man pivoted, revealing a battered badge pinned to his vest. "Hold it right there, mister. I'm Fred Withers, town marshal. You wouldn't happen to know what all that ruckus was about, would you?"

Not breaking stride, Fargo looked straight at Luther Keller. "Someone tried to kill me."

Murmuring broke out, which the lawman hushed with

a sharp gesture. "You don't say? Suppose we go to my office and you give me the details."

Fargo walked past Withers to the Ovaro. "Suppose you join me in the saloon and I'll tell you about it over my meal." He checked to insure the slug hadn't nicked the pinto, then stroked its neck, deciding to leave it tied to the hitch rail for the time being.

Most of the onlookers were gazing at Withers, awaiting his response. "I reckon that's all right by me," he said.

Fargo had learned two important things about the lawman. One, Withers had less backbone than a snail. Why else had he stayed out in the street when he should have been investigating the gunfire? Any other town, the tin star would have come on the run, guns at the ready. Two, Withers was easily swayed. Most lawmen would tell Fargo his meal could wait and demand he go with them to the jail.

More whispering erupted as Fargo entered Irish Mike's and reclaimed his seat. Only this time, he turned the chair so he could see the entrance and the door to the kitchen. Whoever had tried to dry gulch him might try again.

Fred Withers walked up, but before he could speak both Irish Mike and Flora were at Fargo's side talking at once.

"Who would want to make wolf meat of you, boyo?" the barkeep asked.

"Are you all right, big man? I can hold off on the food if it's spoiled your appetite," Flora offered.

Fargo took a swig of whiskey, then wiped his mouth with the back of his sleeve. "I don't know who shot at me. And I'm still hungry enough to eat a buffalo raw, so bring on those eggs, my dear."

As Flannigan and the proprietor moved off, the lawman pulled out a chair, saying, "I guess that answers my most important question. But I don't much like lead being slung in our streets. I run a quiet town, mister. On the weekend some of the miners can be a mite rowdy, but by and large Silver Flats is as peaceful as can be. There hasn't been a gunfight in a coon's age."

"It must make your job a lot easier," Fargo said.

Withers nodded. "And that's how I like it. Easy as can be. I don't much like gents who stir up trouble."

"Tell that to the bastard who tried to blow out my wick."

The lawman held up both hands, palms out. "I'm not accusing you of any wrongdoing. I'm just stating my policy. Which is why I'm afraid I'll have to ask you to leave town as soon as you're done eating."

Fargo thought about Keller and Harvey and Pardee. In his mind's eye, he then relived the moment when the rifleman fired at him from the roof. He recalled all too vividly how close he had come to being planted in an unmarked grave in the town cemetery. "No," he said.

Withers blinked. "No?"

"You heard me."

"But *you* must not have heard *me*. I'm not asking you, mister. I'm telling you. I want you out of Silver Flats. Whoever you are, you've brought trouble. Take it somewhere else. That's as plain as I can be."

"The answer is still no."

The lawman gnawed on his lower lip. At length he said, "I can deputize all the men I need to make you leave, whether you want to or not. There's still ten or eleven in town—more than enough to handle the likes of you."

"You won't, though."

"What makes you so sure?"

"You just said you don't like trouble. And if you try to throw me out, you'll have more trouble than a rat in a viper's nest." Fargo leaned on his elbows. "Since you laid your cards on the table, I'll do the same. I'm not going anywhere until I find out who tried to kill me and why."

"Listen," Withers said defensively, "you can't just ride on in here and act like you're the cock of the roost. We abide by the letter of the law."

Fargo was tired of his carping. "Is it against the law for me to stay as long as I want?" he demanded.

"Technically, no, but—"

"Then you're wasting your breath. Go pester someone else. Or, better yet, track down the man who shot at me and I'll be out of your hair that much sooner." Fargo extended the bottle. "Care for a drink before you go?"

Peeved, Withers shoved his chair back and stood. "I don't think I much like you very much, mister. You can stick around for now, though. If there's any more gunplay, however, you'll regret being so pushy. I'll only bend so far."

"That's good to hear," Fargo said, and meant it.

No sooner had the lawman tromped off than Flora swayed out, bearing a coffeepot and a cup and saucer on a tray. "The eggs will be ready in a minute." She set the tray down, regarding him with lively interest. "Tell me, big man. Do you have a place to stay tonight?"

"Not yet. Why?"

Flora bent so her luscious mouth was inches from his. "I happen to have a spare room which you're more than welcome to use. Interested?"

"Very much so," Fargo replied, marveling at the turn of events. He remembered thinking that Silver Flats must be dull. How wrong he'd been. In less than an hour someone had tried to murder him and a lovely woman was inviting him to spend the night.

What next?